HOW TO WRITE BESTSELLING ROMANTIC SUSPENSE

FROM FIRST KISS TO FINAL SHOWDOWN

JUST BAE

CONTENTS

1

UNDERSTANDING ROMANTIC SUSPENSE

The Essence of Romantic Suspense

Romantic suspense is a captivating hybrid genre that intertwines the thrills of suspense with the emotional depth of romance. At its core, this genre features a central love story that is not merely a backdrop but a pivotal plot component. As characters navigate the complexities of their relationships, they are also thrust into a world filled with danger and intrigue, creating a compelling narrative that keeps readers on the edge of their seats.

A defining characteristic of romantic suspense is a suspenseful storyline marked by high stakes. These stakes often manifest in situations that threaten the characters' lives or emotional well-being, such as murder investigations, conspiracies, or hidden identities. For example, a detective may fall in love with a witness to a crime, only to discover her life is in imminent danger. This scenario heightens tension and intensifies the romantic connection as the detective races against time to protect her.

Fast pacing is another hallmark of this genre, propelling the narrative forward and ensuring reader engagement. The story alternates between heart-pounding moments of suspense and intimate scenes that explore the characters' evolving relationship. This rhythmic balance allows readers to catch their breath while remaining emotionally invested in the characters' journey.

Moreover, complex characters with emotional depth are essential in romantic suspense. Protagonists should possess strong motivations, relatable flaws, and relevant skills that drive the plot and enhance romantic tension. For instance, a skilled hacker might find herself in peril while uncovering a conspiracy, forcing her love interest, a rugged former military operative, to confront his own fears and vulnerabilities. Their growth as individuals and as a couple adds richness to the narrative.

Plot twists are vital elements that keep readers guessing and contribute to the resolution of both romantic and suspenseful arcs. Unexpected turns, such as betrayal from a trusted ally or the revelation of a hidden past, heighten suspense and deepen emotional stakes, making the resolution more satisfying.

In essence, romantic suspense weaves a central love story with an engaging suspense plot, characterized by high stakes, fast pacing, complex characters, and unexpected twists. By mastering these elements, writers can create gripping narratives that captivate readers and fulfill their expectations for both romance and suspense.

Balancing Acts

Achieving a harmonious blend of romance and suspense is essential for a successful romantic suspense novel. The interplay between these elements should feel natural and seamless, enhancing the narrative rather than competing with one another. A well-crafted story captivates readers with romantic entanglements while keeping them on the edge of their seats with suspenseful twists.

To maintain this balance, writers can employ several key strategies:

Alternating Between Romantic and Suspenseful Scenes: One effective approach is to alternate between romantic and suspenseful scenes, allowing moments of tension to lead into emotional intimacy. For example, envision a scene where the protagonists escape a perilous situation. The adrenaline of their escape can heighten their emotional connection, culminating in a tender moment where they finally express their feelings. This interplay deepens their relationship and keeps readers engaged in both romance and suspense.

Using Quiet Moments for Character Development: While the story may be filled with action and tension, it's crucial to carve out quiet moments for character development. These interludes allow readers to witness the growth of the relationship amid chaos. For instance, a scene where characters share a quiet dinner can reveal their vulnerabilities, providing a stark contrast to the external threats they face. Such moments offer a breather for the reader while reinforcing the emotional stakes of the romance.

Creating Genuine Danger: The stakes in a romantic suspense novel should feel real and immediate. This can be achieved by placing characters in genuine danger that forces them into close proximity. For instance, a murder investigation might compel the protagonists to work together, heightening their emotional connection as they rely on each other for safety. The shared experience of overcoming danger can intensify their bond, making their romance feel organic and authentic.

Incorporating Conflicts from Both Romance and Suspense: The integration of conflicts from both the romantic and suspense elements leads to complex character interactions and growth. For example, if one character hides a secret that could jeopardize their relationship while being pursued by a mysterious antagonist, the tension creates a rich tapestry of emotional conflict. This duality allows characters to confront their fears and uncertainties, ultimately strengthening their connection as they navigate challenges together.

By focusing on these strategies, writers can create a romantic suspense novel that resonates with readers and meets their expectations for both genres. The balance of romance and suspense is not merely a stylistic choice; it is the heartbeat of the story, driving the narrative forward and inviting readers to immerse themselves in a world where love and danger intertwine.

Reader Expectations

Understanding what readers seek in a romantic suspense novel is crucial for crafting a compelling story that resonates deeply with its audience. The unique blend of romance and suspense creates a multifaceted experience, and meeting reader expectations is key to ensuring they remain engaged from the first page to the last. Below are the primary expectations that aspiring writers should keep in mind when developing their romantic suspense narratives.

A Satisfying Romantic Arc: At the heart of every romantic suspense novel lies a central love story that must develop naturally alongside the suspense plot. Readers expect a romantic arc that feels genuine and evolves with the characters. The growth of the relationship should mirror the escalating tension of the suspenseful elements. For instance, if protagonists are embroiled in a dangerous conspiracy, their shared experiences should forge a bond that deepens with each challenge. A well-crafted romantic arc enhances emotional stakes and enriches suspense, making both elements more impactful.

High Stakes with Personal Connections: Readers are drawn to stories where the stakes feel personal and significant. In romantic suspense, this often translates to situations that directly affect the main characters. Whether it's a loved one in danger or a personal vendetta, the stakes should be high enough to keep readers on edge. For example, if the protagonist is a detective investigating murders, and the love interest turns out to be a key witness, the intertwining of their fates raises tension dramatically. This connection propels the plot while ensuring readers are emotionally invested in the outcome.

Authenticity in Suspenseful Situations: Authenticity is paramount in creating a believable world for readers. This includes realistic portrayals of suspenseful situations such as murder investigations, conspiracies, or hidden identities. Readers expect writers to conduct thorough research, ensuring that procedures, settings, and character actions are credible. For instance, if your plot involves a forensic investigation, providing accurate details about crime scene protocols can enhance realism and immerse readers in the narrative.

Resolution for Both Narratives: A satisfying conclusion is essential in romantic suspense. Readers anticipate a resolution that ties up both the romantic and suspense threads of the story. This means delivering an ending where the romantic relationship reaches a fulfilling conclusion while also resolving the suspense plot logically. For instance, if protagonists have faced numerous threats, readers will expect a climax that resolves danger and allows characters to confront their feelings for one another.

Engaging Writing with a Fast Pace: Finally, engaging writing is a cornerstone of any successful romantic suspense novel. Readers crave a narrative that maintains a fast pace, ensuring that both romance and suspense elements progress simultaneously. Techniques such as short, punchy chapters, cliffhangers, and alternating perspectives can keep momentum going. A well-paced story captivates readers and amplifies tension, making each twist and turn exhilarating.

By focusing on these elements, writers can create a romantic suspense novel that not only meets but exceeds reader expectations. The successful integration of romance and suspense, combined with compelling character development and a gripping plot, will ensure that readers are left yearning for more long after they turn the final page.

2

CREATING COMPELLING CHARACTERS

Protagonists and Antagonists

In romantic suspense, the protagonists and antagonists are crucial to the story's appeal. These characters drive the narrative, making their development essential for a gripping and emotionally resonant tale.

The protagonist, whether hero or heroine, should be multifaceted, with strong motivations that propel them through the unfolding drama. Readers are drawn to authentic characters, often shaped by relatable flaws. For instance, a protagonist with a past marked by betrayal may grapple with trust issues that complicate their budding romance. This internal conflict humanizes them and cultivates tension in the love story. Consider a detective haunted by a previous case; their journey to find love intertwines with their quest for redemption, adding depth to both their personal and romantic arcs.

Equally important is the antagonist, who should never be a mere caricature of evil. This character must have motivations and goals that oppose those of the protagonist. A well-crafted antagonist might be a former ally turned rival, a shadowy figure with a personal vendetta, or someone whose ambitions threaten the protagonist's happiness. For example, envision a corrupt official with a vested interest in the protagonist's investigation. Such a character creates external conflict and challenges the protagonist's moral compass, forcing them to confront their own values and choices.

The interplay between these two characters is vital. When both are developed with depth, their conflict transcends a simple plot device; it evolves into a dynamic relationship that captivates the reader. The protagonist's journey to overcome the antagonist's obstacles can mirror their emotional journey in romance, creating a cohesive narrative that resonates on multiple levels.

To achieve this complexity, authors should craft detailed backstories for both the protagonist and antagonist. These backstories should illuminate their motivations, fears, and desires, allowing readers to understand their actions. For example, a protagonist who once trusted the antagonist as a friend may face a gut-wrenching betrayal that fuels the suspense and complicates their romantic entanglements.

This layered storytelling invites readers to invest emotionally in the characters' journeys.

In summary, the protagonists and antagonists in a romantic suspense novel must be intricately woven into the story. By giving them relatable flaws, strong motivations, and complex backstories, authors create characters that are engaging and essential to the unfolding drama. These dynamic relationships propel the narrative forward, ensuring readers are captivated by both the suspense and romance that define the genre.

Love Interests

In romantic suspense, the love interest is not merely a side character; they are a vital counterpart to the protagonist, enriching the narrative with their own complexities and driving the emotional core of the story. To create a compelling love interest, authors must ensure that these characters are as fully realized and multifaceted as the protagonist. This balance fosters a partnership that feels authentic and engaging, heightening the stakes of both the romantic and suspenseful elements of the plot.

A well-developed love interest should possess skills and attributes that complement the protagonist's character. This synergy enhances their partnership and propels the plot. For instance, if the protagonist is a detective with a keen analytical mind, their love interest might be a forensic expert whose insights lead to crucial breakthroughs in the investigation. This dynamic cultivates teamwork and mutual respect, deepening their connection while advancing the narrative.

Moreover, the love interest should have their own aspirations and motivations that may conflict with those of the protagonist. Such tension can arise from professional rivalries, differing moral compasses, or personal stakes that complicate their relationship. For example, if the love interest is an undercover agent working against a criminal organization that the protagonist is investigating, the potential for betrayal and mistrust can add layers of intrigue and emotional depth to their interactions.

Chemistry between the protagonist and their love interest is essential for drawing readers into the romance. This chemistry should be palpable and developed through shared experiences, playful banter, and moments of vulnerability. Authors can showcase their growing attraction through dialogue that reflects their unique personalities and the tension inherent in their situation. A witty exchange during a high-stress moment can highlight their compatibility, while a tender moment of support during a crisis can reveal their emotional depth.

As the relationship evolves, it's important to portray the transition from initial attraction to deeper emotional connections. This journey can be facilitated by moments that test their bond, such as facing external threats that compel them to rely on one another. These experiences heighten the stakes and allow for the gradual unveiling of vulnerabilities, fostering trust and intimacy.

An effective romantic arc must include obstacles that challenge the love interest's relationship with the protagonist. Conflicts can stem from personal histories, such as unresolved traumas or past relationships. For example, if the love interest harbors deep-seated trust issues due to a previous betrayal, this can create friction as they navigate their new relationship. The protagonist's attempts to reassure and prove their sincerity can lead to poignant moments of growth and understanding.

Additionally, external pressures—such as threats from an antagonist—can complicate their romance. The love interest may find themselves torn between their feelings for the protagonist and their own safety, creating palpable tension that keeps readers invested. This interplay of internal and external conflicts enriches the romantic storyline and intertwines it seamlessly with the suspense elements of the plot.

The love interest in a romantic suspense novel should be a dynamic character in their own right, equipped with complementary skills, complex motivations, and compelling chemistry with the protagonist. By skillfully navigating the intricacies of their relationship, authors can create a romance that resonates deeply with readers, enhancing the overall impact of the narrative and ensuring that both the romantic and suspenseful arcs are equally engaging.

Supporting Cast

In romantic suspense, supporting characters are not merely background figures; they are vital threads that weave through the narrative, enriching the story and enhancing the emotional depth of the protagonists. Each secondary character should be crafted with care, possessing distinct personality traits and clear roles that contribute meaningfully to the plot. Their interactions with the main characters illuminate themes of loyalty, betrayal, and personal growth, creating a more immersive experience for the reader.

A well-developed supporting cast serves multiple purposes. These characters can act as confidants, providing the protagonist with a sounding board for their fears and desires. Consider a wise mentor who has faced similar challenges; their guidance can help the hero or heroine navigate the treacherous waters of both romance and suspense. This mentor might have a military background, offering insights that are relevant to the plot and grounded in authenticity.

Moreover, secondary characters can serve as foils to the main characters, highlighting their strengths and weaknesses. Imagine a best friend who embodies carefree spontaneity, contrasting sharply with the protagonist's serious demeanor. This dynamic can create moments of levity, providing relief from the tension of the suspenseful plot while showcasing the protagonist's internal conflicts and growth. For instance, as the protagonist grapples with trust issues stemming from a past betrayal, the friend's unwavering support can remind them of the importance of vulnerability in relationships.

In addition to serving as confidants and foils, supporting characters can introduce subplots that parallel the main romance, adding layers to the narrative. A romantic subplot involving a secondary character can mirror the primary relationship, reinforcing themes of love and connection. For example, if the protagonist's friend finds themselves in a budding romance with a character who has a murky past, it can create tension and intrigue that resonates with the main plot. This parallel storyline enhances the emotional stakes, making the primary romance feel more urgent and compelling.

It is crucial to avoid stereotypes when developing these characters. Each supporting character should possess unique traits and backstories that make them relatable and memorable. For instance, instead of the typical comic relief character who exists solely for humor, consider creating a character with a rich history that informs their actions and decisions. Perhaps this character has faced their own challenges, such as overcoming addiction or dealing with loss, which can add depth to their interactions and influence the main characters' journeys.

Finally, the relationships between the supporting cast and the protagonists can reflect the central themes of the story. Through their interactions, readers can witness the evolution of loyalty, betrayal, and personal growth. A supportive friend may challenge the protagonist to confront their fears, while a rival character may force them to question their motivations and desires. These dynamics enrich the narrative and allow readers to engage more deeply with the characters' emotional arcs.

In summary, the supporting cast in a romantic suspense novel is vital to creating a well-rounded story. By developing secondary characters with distinct personalities, relevant backstories, and meaningful roles, writers can enhance the depth and complexity of their narratives. These characters should not only serve the plot but also contribute to the emotional landscape of the story, making the protagonists' journey more resonant and impactful. Through their interactions, themes of love, trust, and personal growth can be explored, allowing readers to connect with the characters on a profound level.

3

CRAFTING A GRIPPING SUSPENSE PLOT

Starting with a Hook

In romantic suspense, the opening hook is not just an introduction; it's a vital lifeline that draws readers into your narrative. A powerful hook captures attention instantly, setting the stage for a thrilling journey filled with pulse-pounding suspense and emotional depth. To craft an effective hook, consider introducing an intriguing scenario, a compelling character, or an unexpected event right from the first page.

Imagine starting your novel with a character teetering on the edge of a cliff, heart racing as they witness a crime unfold below. This vivid imagery immerses readers in the scene, allowing them to feel the protagonist's adrenaline. Alternatively, you might introduce a mysterious phone call delivering shocking news, leaving both the character and the reader in suspense. This approach captivates and fore-shadows the themes and conflicts that will intertwine throughout the story.

An effective hook should also establish the tone of your narrative. If your story leans dark and intense, consider beginning with a chilling action scene that heightens the stakes. For instance, a character might find themselves being chased through a dimly lit alley, relying solely on their instincts. This creates urgency and hints at the challenges ahead as the plot unfolds.

Remember, the hook must do more than attract attention; it should lay the groundwork for both the suspense and romance elements of your story. A well-crafted opening can suggest the emotional turmoil the characters will endure while introducing the suspenseful plot that keeps readers on the edge of their seats.

As you develop your hook, consider the questions you want your readers to ponder. What is at stake for the characters? What secrets are they concealing? By igniting curiosity, you encourage readers to keep turning the pages, eager to unravel the mysteries woven into your narrative.

Starting with a strong hook is essential for capturing your reader's attention and establishing the tone for your romantic suspense novel. By presenting a compelling situation, character, or event that hints at the themes and conflicts to come, you create an irresistible invitation for readers to delve deeper into your crafted world. The journey begins here—make it unforgettable.

Building Tension

Tension is the lifeblood of a gripping suspense plot, intricately woven into the narrative from the very first page. As a writer in the romantic suspense genre, your aim is to create an atmosphere of urgency and danger that keeps readers engaged while exploring the complexities of love. Here are several techniques to effectively build tension throughout your story.

Start Early with a Sense of Danger

Begin your narrative with a palpable sense of danger or urgency. Introduce a precarious situation—perhaps your protagonist is fleeing from an unseen threat or uncovering a shocking secret. For example, consider opening with your heroine receiving a cryptic message warning her of impending peril, immediately raising the stakes and compelling readers to turn the page.

Introduce High Stakes

Ensure the stakes are high and personally relevant to your characters, making readers emotionally invested in the outcome. Imagine a scenario where your main character is not only solving a murder but also protecting a loved one who may be the next target. Intertwining the characters' personal lives with the overarching suspense creates a narrative that resonates deeply with readers.

Employ Cliffhangers and Alternating Perspectives

To maintain a fast pace and keep readers engaged, utilize cliffhangers at the end of chapters. This technique leaves readers hungry for resolution, compelling them to continue reading. For example, conclude a chapter with your protagonist discovering crucial evidence just as they hear footsteps approaching, leaving readers breathless with anticipation.

Additionally, consider alternating perspectives between characters. This method reveals different pieces of information, creating a layered narrative that enhances suspense. As readers gain insights into various characters' thoughts and motivations, they become more invested in the unfolding drama.

Layer in Subplots and Action Scenes

Incorporating subplots can complicate the main storyline and add depth. Perhaps your protagonist is navigating a complicated romantic relationship while trying to solve the central mystery. This dual focus enriches character development and raises tension as readers witness how romance is affected by the suspenseful plot.

Periodic action scenes are crucial for maintaining a brisk pace. These moments of heightened excitement can range from a chase through darkened streets to a tense confrontation in a secluded location. For instance, a scene where the hero confronts a suspect in a dimly lit warehouse can elevate adrenaline levels while advancing both the suspense and romantic arcs.

Incorporate Countdown or Deadlines

Using countdowns or deadlines can significantly heighten urgency in your story. Imagine your protagonist has only 48 hours to uncover the truth before a loved one is put in danger. This ticking clock creates pressure that propels your narrative forward, compelling characters to act swiftly and making readers anxious to see what happens next.

By employing these techniques, you will create a narrative that is both suspenseful and rich in emotional stakes. The tension you build will seamlessly intertwine with the romantic elements of your story, ensuring that readers are fully engaged and invested in both the characters and their journey. As you craft your gripping suspense plot, remember that success lies in maintaining a delicate balance between building tension and exploring the complexities of love.

Incorporating Plot Twists

In romantic suspense, plot twists propel the story forward and keep readers on the edge of their seats. These unexpected turns enhance suspense and deepen the romantic elements, intertwining the two genres in a captivating way.

The Art of Deception: Introducing Red Herrings

To maintain mystery, introduce multiple suspects or red herrings that divert attention from the true culprit. For instance, if your protagonist is embroiled in a murder investigation, consider presenting a seemingly innocent character with hidden secrets. This could be a charming neighbor with a past, a co-worker with a questionable alibi, or a family member whose loyalty is in question. Layering these suspects creates an intricate web of intrigue that encourages readers to question everything they think they know.

Foreshadowing: The Subtle Hint

Foreshadowing allows you to plant clues that hint at future developments without revealing too much. For example, if your protagonist discovers an old photograph linking her love interest to a past crime, this hint creates tension and anticipation. As readers progress, they'll piece together clues, leading to a satisfying "aha" moment when the truth is revealed. This technique keeps readers engaged and enriches the romantic subplot, adding layers of complexity to the characters' relationship.

Surprise Revelations: The Moment of Shock

Strategically placed surprise revelations can lead to moments of shock that force readers to reevaluate earlier events. Imagine revealing that the protagonist's love interest is not just a charming stranger but has been secretly investigating her family's dark past. This twist heightens suspense and complicates the romantic relationship, introducing elements of betrayal and trust that must be navigated. Such revelations create emotional turmoil, compelling characters to confront their feelings and motivations.

Crafting a Satisfying Resolution

As you weave these twists into your narrative, ensure that both the romantic and suspense plots culminate in a satisfying ending. Readers should feel that the twists align with the story's development and character arcs. For instance, if the love interest's hidden identity is revealed, it should resonate with the protagonist's journey, leading to a resolution that feels earned and authentic. A well-crafted ending will leave readers shocked by the twists and fulfilled by the characters' emotional growth.

Incorporating plot twists in your romantic suspense novel is essential for creating a gripping narrative that captivates readers. By introducing red herrings, employing foreshadowing, delivering surprise revelations, and ensuring a satisfying resolution, you can craft a story that keeps readers guessing while deepening the emotional stakes of the romance. With each twist and turn, draw your audience deeper into the world you've created, ensuring they are fully invested in both the suspense and the love story unfolding before them.

4

THE ARC OF ROMANCE

Stages of Romance Development

The romantic arc in a suspense novel unfolds through a series of compelling stages, each building upon the last to create a rich tapestry of attraction, conflict, and emotional growth. At the heart of this arc lies the initial meeting, a pivotal moment that ignites the spark between the protagonists. This encounter sets the groundwork for their connection, whether it's a chance meeting in a crowded café or a dramatic rescue during a perilous situation. The circumstances of their first interaction should be memorable, signaling to readers that this relationship is destined to evolve.

As the story progresses, characters enter a stage of growing awareness, becoming increasingly conscious of their feelings for one another. This awareness can be illustrated through subtle glances exchanged across a room, shared laughter during tense moments, or emotional responses to each other's actions. For instance, imagine a scene where the heroine witnesses the hero's bravery in a life-threatening scenario; her admiration blossoms into something deeper, allowing readers to feel the shift in her heart.

The next crucial element is sexual tension, which intensifies as the characters interact. This tension often manifests in charged situations that force them into close proximity—perhaps they find themselves hiding together in a darkened alley, their breaths quickening as danger looms. Such scenarios enable readers to sense the underlying attraction, creating a palpable energy that keeps them turning pages. The tension should escalate gradually, moving from innocent touches to more intimate encounters, allowing anticipation to grow organically.

Building trust is essential in this genre, particularly as the suspense unfolds. Characters must learn to rely on one another amid chaos, revealing their vulnerabilities and fears. For example, if the hero has a troubled past that affects his ability to open up, his gradual willingness to share these secrets with the heroine deepens their bond. This trust forms the foundation of their relationship, transforming it into something more than a fleeting romance.

As emotional intimacy develops, characters share their fears, aspirations, and dreams, fostering a connection critical for a satisfying relationship arc. This stage is not without challenges; conflicts and setbacks often arise, testing the strength of their bond. These obstacles can be external, such as a looming threat from an antagonist, or internal, like personal doubts that surface as the characters grow closer. For instance, if the heroine is haunted by a past betrayal, her struggle to trust the hero can create tension that enriches their dynamic.

Ultimately, the arc culminates in resolution and commitment. Here, characters confront their challenges, affirming their relationship in a manner that intertwines both romantic and suspense elements. This resolution should feel earned, allowing for character growth and a satisfying conclusion. Picture a scene where, after overcoming a life-threatening ordeal together, the hero and heroine stand side by side, pledging their commitment to one another as the dust settles. This moment not only resolves their romantic tension but also reinforces the theme of trust and partnership woven throughout the narrative.

In summary, the stages of romance development in a romantic suspense novel are integral to crafting a compelling story. By carefully navigating the initial spark of attraction, building awareness and sexual tension, fostering trust and emotional intimacy, and ultimately resolving conflicts, writers can create a rich romantic arc that captivates readers and enhances the suspenseful narrative. Each stage should feel authentic and connected to the characters' journeys, ensuring that the romance is not merely an addition but a vital component of the overall story.

Techniques to Show Attraction

In romantic suspense, effectively conveying attraction between characters is essential for crafting a compelling love story that resonates with readers. The chemistry shared by the protagonists enhances the romantic arc and intertwines seamlessly with the suspenseful elements of the narrative. Here are several techniques to illustrate this attraction authentically and powerfully.

1. Chemistry Through Dialogue and Interaction:

Dialogue serves as a potent tool for showcasing attraction. Characters should engage in conversations that reveal their feelings organically. Imagine a scene where the protagonists find themselves in close quarters during a tense moment, perhaps hiding from a pursuer. Their dialogue might be laced with playful banter, underscoring their attraction while heightening the suspense. A line like, "You know, if we survive this, I might just owe you a drink," conveys both flirtation and urgency.

2. Internal Monologue:

Utilizing internal monologue allows readers to delve into a character's thoughts and emotions, providing insight into their attraction and internal conflicts. For example, a character might reflect on the other's bravery in a dangerous situation, thinking, "I've never met anyone who could face danger with such calm. It makes me want to know them more." This technique highlights their attraction and deepens the reader's understanding of the character's emotional landscape.

3. Creating Intimate Moments Amid Danger:

The juxtaposition of danger and intimacy can amplify romantic tension. Picture a near-miss scenario where characters narrowly escape a threat, only to find themselves in a secluded location. The shared adrenaline can lead to a breathless moment where they lock eyes, creating a charged atmosphere. Such moments can be pivotal, as the tension from their perilous situation enhances their emotional connection.

4. Gradually Building Sexual Tension:

Sexual tension should evolve naturally throughout the narrative. Start with innocent touches—a brush of hands or a fleeting glance—and gradually escalate to more charged interactions. For instance, during a moment of vulnerability, one character might instinctively reach out to comfort the other, their fingers lingering just a moment too long. This slow build allows readers to feel the anticipation, making the eventual culmination of their attraction all the more satisfying.

5. Recognizing Emotional and Physical Attraction:

It's essential to portray both emotional and physical attraction. Characters should acknowledge not only their physical appeal but also their emotional connection. A character might admire their love interest's determination in the face of danger while simultaneously being drawn to their physical presence. This duality enriches the romantic arc, making the relationship feel multi-dimensional and genuine.

6. Realistic Conflicts Amplifying Attraction:

The circumstances surrounding the characters can amplify their attraction. For example, if they are both trapped in a high-stakes situation, the stress can force them to confront their feelings head-on. A scene where they argue over a plan of action could lead to an unexpected moment of vulnerability, where one character admits, "I can't lose you. Not now." Such conflicts should feel authentic and tied to their journey, making their bond resonate with readers.

By employing these techniques, writers can effectively illustrate the attraction between characters, creating a rich tapestry of emotions that enhances both the romantic and suspenseful elements of their stories. The interplay of danger and desire captivates readers and ensures that the romantic arc remains integral to the overall narrative, paving the way for a satisfying resolution that honors the complexities of love amidst suspense.

Navigating Emotional Complexities

In romantic suspense, the emotional intricacies of a relationship can be as compelling as the external dangers threatening the characters. Navigating these emotional complexities is essential for crafting a believable and engaging romantic arc that resonates with readers. As the protagonists confront perilous situations, their emotional landscape becomes fertile ground for trust issues, internal conflicts, and dynamics that deepen their connection while heightening the stakes.

Trust Issues and Past Traumas

Trust forms the foundation of any romantic relationship, and within a suspenseful context, it can serve as both a challenge and a catalyst for growth. Characters often carry the weight of past traumas that influence their ability to connect with others. For instance, if one character has experienced betrayal in a previous relationship, they may find it difficult to open up to their love interest, creating palpable tension. This internal conflict enriches the character's backstory and presents a barrier that must be overcome for the relationship to flourish. As the suspense unfolds, moments of vulnerability—such as sharing fears or admitting past mistakes—can lead to breakthroughs, allowing the characters to build trust and intimacy.

Internal Conflicts and Moral Dilemmas

The emotional journey of characters in romantic suspense is frequently fraught with internal conflicts mirroring the external dangers they face. A character might grapple with a moral dilemma: should they prioritize their safety or protect their partner at all costs? This conflict adds depth to the narrative, compelling characters to confront their values and make difficult choices that impact their relationship. The tension generated by these dilemmas heightens the suspense and enriches the romantic storyline. Readers become invested in the characters' struggles, rooting for them to find common ground and emerge stronger together.

Relationship Conflicts and Background Differences

The intersection of differing backgrounds and opposing viewpoints can create rich conflict within a romantic relationship. For example, if one protagonist comes from privilege while the other has faced significant hardships, their contrasting perspectives can lead to misunderstandings and tension. These conflicts should feel personal and tied to the characters' journeys, allowing for growth and deeper understanding. As they navigate their differences, moments of connection—like a shared laugh amid chaos or a heartfelt conversation during a quiet moment—can bridge the gap, reinforcing their bond and commitment.

Personal Obstacles and External Threats

In romantic suspense, obstacles often arise from both personal and external sources. External threats—such as a looming danger or a mysterious antagonist—force characters to rely on each other, testing their commitment and resilience. A near-miss situation where characters narrowly escape danger can lead to a breathless moment of intimacy, where they confront their feelings amid the chaos. These shared experiences deepen their emotional connection and emphasize the stakes of their relationship. The resolution of these conflicts should feel earned, allowing characters to grow and evolve in ways that enhance the overall narrative.

Earned Resolutions

As the story unfolds, the resolution of emotional conflicts should naturally culminate from the characters' journeys. Readers crave a satisfying conclusion where the protagonists confront their challenges and affirm their relationship. This can manifest in a powerful moment of connection—perhaps a heartfelt confession during a climactic scene—that intertwines the romantic and suspenseful elements. The emotional resolution should resonate with the reader, reflecting the growth and transformation of the characters while reinforcing the theme of love prevailing against all odds.

In summary, navigating the emotional complexities of a romantic relationship within suspense is crucial for crafting a compelling narrative. By exploring trust issues, internal conflicts, relationship dynamics, and the interplay of personal and external obstacles, writers can create an engaging romantic arc that captivates readers. The journey of love, fraught with challenges and growth, becomes an integral part of the suspenseful tapestry, ensuring that the romance is believable and deeply intertwined with the characters' struggles and triumphs.

5

STRUCTURING YOUR NOVEL

A successful romantic suspense novel typically follows a foundational structure that guides the narrative through its essential phases. This framework captivates readers and ensures that the romantic and suspenseful arcs are intricately woven together, creating a seamless and engaging story.

The journey begins with a compelling hook that draws readers in. This opening scene should introduce the main characters and hint at the central conflict, setting the stage for the unfolding drama. For instance, imagine a determined investigative journalist stumbling upon a chilling crime scene while covering a seemingly innocuous story. This moment grabs attention and foreshadows the intertwining of her professional and personal life, thrusting her into a world filled with danger and unexpected romance.

Following the hook, the inciting incident serves as the catalyst for the story, introducing the primary conflict that drives the narrative forward. Whether it's a murder investigation, a stalker threatening the protagonist's safety, or a conspiracy linking her personal and professional realms, this event must be impactful. For example, a phone call revealing that a close friend has gone missing can thrust the protagonist into a frantic search, intertwining her fate with that of her love interest, who may have a hidden agenda.

As the story progresses, the rising action unfolds as a tapestry of escalating stakes and tension. This phase is crucial for layering in subplots that enhance both the romance and suspense, allowing them to build upon one another. Consider a scenario where the protagonist and her love interest are forced to work together, uncovering clues that deepen their bond while heightening the threats surrounding them. Each revelation should elevate the stakes, leading to moments of vulnerability that enrich their romantic connection.

The midpoint twist is a pivotal turning point that adds complexity to both the romantic relationship and the suspense plot. This twist introduces new information or challenges that alter the characters' trajectories. For instance, discovering that the love interest is connected to the antagonist can create a rift in their relationship, forcing the protagonist to question her trust and feelings. This twist not only propels the narrative forward but also deepens the emotional stakes.

Every gripping story must have a dark moment—a low point where characters confront their greatest fears and doubts. This moment is essential for character development and emotional engagement. Picture the protagonist, overwhelmed by the threats surrounding her and the betrayal she feels, contemplating whether to abandon her search for the truth. This internal conflict should resonate with readers, drawing them deeper into the emotional landscape of the narrative.

Finally, the climax delivers a satisfying resolution for both the romantic and suspenseful elements. This culmination should address all major plot points and character journeys, providing clarity on the suspense elements, such as the fate of the antagonist or the resolution of the central mystery. For example, the protagonist might confront the antagonist in a tense showdown that tests her courage while reconciling with her love interest, who has proven his loyalty in the face of danger.

In the resolution, readers should witness the growth and transformation of the characters, showcasing how their relationship has evolved through the challenges they faced together. Elements of surprise or twists can enhance the impact, leaving readers with a lasting impression. Ultimately, the resolution should feel earned and true to the characters' journeys, celebrating their victories and growth while providing a sense of closure that resonates deeply.

By adhering to this structure, writers can craft a romantic suspense novel that captivates readers from the first page to the last, ensuring that both the romance and suspense elements are intricately balanced and satisfyingly resolved.

Techniques for Effective Pacing

Pacing is vital in crafting a compelling romantic suspense novel. It serves as the heartbeat of your story, keeping readers engaged while balancing the tension of suspense with the emotional depth of romance. To achieve this balance, consider the following techniques to maintain rhythm and momentum throughout your narrative.

Alternating Between Romantic and Suspense Scenes

One effective strategy for pacing is to alternate between romantic and suspenseful scenes. This technique maintains tension while providing readers with moments of emotional connection. For instance, after a high-stakes chase or a revelation about the antagonist, transition to a quiet scene where the protagonists share a tender moment. This shift gives readers a chance to breathe and deepens their investment in the characters' relationship. The juxtaposition of heart-pounding suspense with intimate interactions creates a dynamic reading experience that keeps audiences turning the pages.

Utilizing Quiet Moments for Character Development

Incorporating quiet moments into your narrative is essential for developing the relationship between your characters. These slower-paced scenes allow for introspection, dialogue, and emotional growth, balancing the fast-paced suspense elements. For example, a scene where the protagonists share a meal, reflect on their fears, or reveal personal secrets can foster intimacy and connection. These moments enrich character arcs and provide context for their motivations, making the stakes feel even higher when danger encroaches.

Seamless Transitions Between Tension and Romance

Natural transitions between romantic and suspenseful scenes are vital for maintaining pacing. Aim for smooth shifts that feel organic rather than jarring. For instance, if a romantic dinner is interrupted by a sudden noise outside, the transition can heighten suspense while keeping the romance at the forefront. Crafting these moments with care ensures that readers remain immersed in the story as they experience the characters' emotional highs and lows alongside the plot's tension.

Simultaneous Progression of Both Plots

Both the romantic arc and the suspense plot should progress simultaneously, intertwined in a way that enhances the overall narrative. As the romance deepens, the stakes in the suspense plot should escalate. For example, as the protagonists grow closer, they may uncover secrets about each other that complicate their relationship while facing external threats that test their bond. This interconnectedness heightens reader engagement and enriches the emotional stakes of both storylines.

Building to Dual Climaxes

Finally, building to dual climaxes is crucial for delivering a satisfying resolution in a romantic suspense novel. Each climax should reflect the characters' growth throughout the narrative, culminating in a thrilling and emotionally resonant conclusion. For instance, as the suspense plot peaks—perhaps with a confrontation with the antagonist—the romantic arc can also reach a critical turning point where the protagonists must confront their feelings for one another. This dual climax creates a powerful moment that resonates with readers, as they experience the culmination of both the suspenseful and romantic journeys.

By employing these pacing techniques, you can create a romantic suspense novel that captivates readers from the first page to the last. The key lies in maintaining a delicate balance between tension and emotional depth, ensuring that both elements progress in harmony for a truly engaging narrative experience.

Ensuring Satisfactory Resolutions

In romantic suspense, the resolution serves as the grand finale, where both the romantic and suspenseful arcs converge to provide readers with a fulfilling conclusion. It is essential that this resolution resonates with the reader, addressing all major plot points while celebrating the characters' journeys through conflict and growth.

A satisfying resolution begins by tying up loose ends, particularly concerning the suspense elements that have driven the narrative. For instance, if your story revolves around a murder investigation, the resolution should clarify the fate of the antagonist, revealing how justice is served. This provides closure and reinforces the stakes established throughout the book. Readers should feel a sense of relief as the mystery unravels, gaining insight into how the pieces fit together.

Simultaneously, the romantic arc must reflect the characters' evolution. Throughout the story, your protagonists have faced challenges that tested their connection. In the resolution, it is crucial to showcase how these trials have transformed their relationship. For example, if your characters began with trust issues stemming from past traumas, the resolution should illustrate their growth—perhaps through a heartfelt conversation that exposes their vulnerabilities and solidifies their bond. This emotional culmination allows readers to feel invested in the characters' happiness and future together.

Moreover, a successful resolution often incorporates elements of surprise or twists that enhance the overall impact of the story. Consider a scenario where the charming love interest is revealed to have a hidden agenda, only to ultimately choose love over deception. This twist provides an unexpected turn and emphasizes the theme of redemption, leaving readers with a lasting impression of character growth.

As you craft your resolution, strive to create a scene that encapsulates both the romantic and suspenseful arcs. This could be a moment of reflection where the protagonists share their thoughts on the journey they've endured, perhaps while overlooking a breathtaking sunset or in the safety of their newfound home. Such imagery heightens the emotional stakes and serves as a visual representation of their journey from chaos to peace.

Finally, ensure that your resolution feels earned and true to the characters' experiences. Avoid rushing to a tidy ending; instead, allow the characters to articulate their feelings and reflect on their journeys. This can be achieved through dialogue that captures their growth or through poignant moments that highlight their shared experiences. For instance, a simple yet powerful exchange of vows or promises can encapsulate their commitment to facing the future together, reinforcing the emotional weight of their relationship.

A well-crafted resolution in romantic suspense is not merely about tying up loose ends; it is about celebrating the characters' growth and providing a sense of closure that resonates with readers. By addressing both the romantic and suspenseful arcs with depth and sincerity, you create a lasting impression that lingers long after the final page is turned.

6

BUILDING TENSION AND CONFLICT

External Conflicts

In romantic suspense, external conflicts drive the narrative and push characters into uncharted emotional territories. These conflicts act as catalysts that heighten the stakes, drawing characters closer together and igniting romantic tension.

Physical danger is a quintessential element that raises these stakes significantly. Consider a determined detective unraveling a murder mystery, only to find themselves cornered by the antagonist they pursue. This palpable threat not only heightens suspense but also compels characters to rely on one another for survival, transforming fear into a powerful bond.

Time pressure serves as another critical external conflict that amplifies both suspense and romance. Imagine a couple racing against the clock to avert a looming disaster. As they navigate their feelings amidst immediate threats, the urgency can lead to profound revelations. The adrenaline rush strips away pretenses, allowing characters to confront their emotions directly. This heightened urgency can result in passionate encounters, where every stolen moment feels charged with significance.

Professional obligations often clash with personal feelings, particularly for characters in law enforcement or investigative roles. For example, a seasoned FBI agent may find themselves torn between their duty to apprehend a suspect and their growing affection for a civilian caught in the crossfire. This dilemma enriches the narrative, forcing the character to confront their priorities and desires.

Outside threats, such as an antagonist's relentless pursuit, can disrupt romance and test relationships. When danger looms, emotional stakes rise, and a character's commitment to their partner may be challenged. Life-threatening situations can lead to moments of doubt and fear, prompting a reassessment of feelings and the strength of their bond.

Competing interests and environmental challenges further complicate the narrative. Picture a couple navigating a treacherous landscape while being pursued by an unseen enemy. The harsh realities of their surroundings can forge intimacy through adversity, compelling them to rely on one another.

Incorporating these elements ensures sustained tension throughout the narrative, keeping readers engaged. The interplay of external conflicts not only propels the plot but also enriches romantic dynamics, creating a compelling story that resonates with audiences. By weaving together physical danger, time pressure, professional dilemmas, and environmental challenges, writers can craft captivating stories that fulfill readers' expectations for both romance and suspense.

Internal Conflicts

Internal conflicts are powerful forces that shape characters in romantic suspense novels. These struggles arise from past experiences, fears, and emotional vulnerabilities, creating a rich tapestry of dilemmas that can either strengthen or fracture relationships. Exploring these complexities allows writers to create characters that resonate deeply with readers.

One significant internal conflict stems from trust issues. Characters often bear the scars of previous relationships, making them hesitant to form new bonds. A protagonist betrayed by a former partner may struggle to open up to a new love interest, fearing history will repeat itself. This tension adds depth to their character and creates a relatable struggle for readers.

Past trauma can further complicate romantic development. A character who has experienced a violent crime or significant loss may grapple with emotional barriers that hinder their ability to embrace new relationships. The journey toward healing becomes pivotal, as the character learns to confront their fears while navigating a thrilling yet dangerous world. For instance, a female detective haunted by past trauma might find herself torn between her feelings for a fellow investigator and the fear of vulnerability that intimacy brings.

Professional ethics and moral dilemmas introduce another layer of internal conflict. Characters often face decisions that pit personal desires against professional responsibilities. Consider a law enforcement officer who develops feelings for a key witness in a murder investigation. The tension mounts as they weigh their duty to uphold the law against their growing affection, creating a poignant struggle that captivates readers.

Family obligations and personal fears also shape characters' decisions. A character caring for a sick parent may hesitate to pursue romance, fearing it will distract them from their responsibilities. This conflict leads to moments of introspection, where they confront their priorities and desires. Personal fears, such as fear of commitment or fear of loss, can further complicate relationships, forcing characters to face their insecurities.

Conflicting goals between characters can lead to misunderstandings and friction, highlighting the importance of communication in relationships. For instance, if one character aims to solve a crime while the other focuses on family protection, their differing priorities can create tension that jeopardizes their bond. This dynamic adds complexity to their relationship and serves as a catalyst for emotional growth.

Internal conflicts enrich character development in romantic suspense novels. By weaving together trust issues, past traumas, professional dilemmas, family obligations, and conflicting goals, writers create multifaceted characters whose emotional journeys resonate with readers. These internal struggles enhance the romantic arc and serve as compelling catalysts for change, leading to a satisfying resolution in both romance and suspense.

Relationship Conflicts

In romantic suspense, relationship conflicts serve as a crucible for character development and emotional depth. These conflicts challenge the romantic bond between protagonists and enrich the narrative, creating a compelling tapestry of struggles that resonate with readers. Skillfully weaving these conflicts into your story is essential for crafting an engaging romantic suspense novel.

One potent source of conflict arises from characters' differing backgrounds and opposing viewpoints. For example, a seasoned detective who falls for a journalist investigating the same case may clash with their professional obligations. The detective prioritizes the investigation, while the journalist, driven to uncover the truth, feels frustrated by the detective's secrecy. This dynamic heightens tension and emphasizes the characters' individual needs and values.

Professional competition can also strain a romantic relationship. Picture two characters on opposing sides of a high-stakes investigation, each convinced of their approach. Their rivalry may manifest in snarky banter, passionate arguments, or attempts to sabotage each other's efforts. This not only raises the stakes professionally but complicates their personal connection, forcing them to confront their feelings amidst chaos.

Trust barriers, often rooted in past relationships, can hinder emotional intimacy. A character betrayed in a previous romance may struggle to open up to a new love interest, fearing vulnerability. This internal conflict can lead to misunderstandings and emotional distance, creating fertile ground for character growth. As the story unfolds, the journey toward rebuilding trust can become a central theme, allowing readers to witness the evolution of the relationship.

Family disapproval can further complicate romantic tension. If one character comes from a family of law enforcement officers while the other is a former criminal, the clash of family values creates significant obstacles. Characters may feel torn between their love and loyalty to family expectations, heightening emotional stakes. This conflict deepens the narrative and provides opportunities for character development as they assert their desires.

Finally, conflicting priorities can exacerbate relationship tensions. A character deeply committed to their career may struggle to find time for romance, leading to feelings of neglect. Conversely, a partner prioritizing personal life may feel unsupported. These dynamics create a rich backdrop for exploration, allowing characters to confront their ambitions and desires while navigating their relationship complexities.

By incorporating these relationship conflicts into your romantic suspense narrative, you create a multi-layered story that captivates readers. Each conflict serves as an obstacle for characters to overcome and a catalyst for their emotional growth. As they navigate the tumultuous waters of love and danger, readers become invested in their journey, eager to see how they resolve their differences and ultimately find their way to each other. This intricate dance of conflict and resolution is what makes romantic suspense thrilling and relatable, ensuring readers are left longing for more.

7

TECHNIQUES FOR WRITING WITH IMPACT

Point of View Choices

In romantic suspense, the choice of point of view (POV) is a powerful tool that enhances the emotional resonance of your narrative. The right POV allows readers to connect deeply with characters, amplifying both the romantic and suspenseful elements of your story.

Dual POV for Depth and Contrast

Utilizing a dual point of view—shifting between the hero and heroine—invites readers into the intimate thoughts and feelings of both main characters. This technique enriches the narrative by offering contrasting perspectives on their evolving relationship and the suspenseful plot. For instance, when the heroine grapples with fear during a tense moment, the hero's viewpoint can reveal his determination to protect her, heightening the emotional stakes. This interplay deepens reader investment and creates a dynamic tension that propels the narrative forward.

Limited Third-Person Deep POV

Another effective approach is the limited third-person deep POV, which immerses readers in a character's experience, granting intimate access to their thoughts and emotions. This technique is particularly impactful in romantic suspense, where understanding a character's internal struggles elevates the stakes. For example, if your protagonist conceals a dark secret while falling in love, the deep POV allows readers to feel their anxiety and excitement, weaving a rich tapestry of emotional complexity. By placing readers directly in the character's mind, you foster a closeness that makes the unfolding drama feel intensely personal.

Alternating Chapters or Scenes

To maintain pacing and tension, consider employing alternating chapters or scenes. This structure provides a rhythm that keeps readers engaged and ensures clarity in POV transitions. When executed well, it allows seamless navigation between perspectives, enabling readers to experience the same event through different lenses. For instance, after a climactic moment where the hero confronts the antagonist, switching to the heroine's POV can reveal her reaction and emotional turmoil, adding layers to the narrative.

In summary, the choice of point of view in your romantic suspense novel is crucial. Whether you opt for dual POVs that showcase contrasting emotions, a deep third-person perspective that immerses readers in intimate thoughts, or alternating chapters that maintain narrative rhythm, each choice should enhance the emotional depth and suspense of your story. By thoughtfully considering how you present your characters' perspectives, you can create a compelling and immersive reading experience.

Scene Structure

Creating a compelling scene structure is essential for maintaining reader engagement in a romantic suspense novel. Each scene should serve multiple purposes—advancing the plot, deepening character development, and enhancing emotional stakes. Here are key techniques to craft effective scenes that resonate with your audience.

Start with Action or Tension

Begin each scene with an element of action or tension to immediately engage readers. This approach hooks the audience from the first line, establishing a dynamic tone. For instance, picture a scene where Claire, the heroine, discovers a mysterious note among her late father's belongings, hinting at hidden danger. This opening sparks curiosity and propels the narrative forward by introducing immediate conflict.

Integrate Plot and Character Development

Every scene should push the plot ahead while revealing deeper layers of character. When Claire confronts her estranged brother about the note, the scene can explore their strained relationship while advancing the mystery. This dual focus ensures that every moment in your story is meaningful, contributing to both the narrative arc and character depth.

End with Hooks

To encourage readers to turn the page, conclude scenes with hooks—cliffhangers or unresolved tensions that create suspense. For example, as Claire and her brother argue, he might unveil a shocking secret about their father's past, leaving readers eager to learn more. This technique effectively propels readers into the next chapter, maintaining momentum throughout the novel.

Vary Pace and Intensity

Keep readers on their toes by varying the pace and intensity of scenes. Alternating between high-stakes action and quieter, introspective moments allows for emotional processing and character growth. A thrilling chase through a dark alley can be followed by a tender moment where Claire reflects on her feelings for the detective assisting her. This ebb and flow of tension creates a rhythm that keeps readers engaged.

Balance Dialogue and Description

Striking a balance between dialogue and description is crucial for immersing readers in your story. Dialogue reveals character personality and advances the plot, while description sets the scene and evokes mood. For instance, as Claire and the detective discuss their next move, vivid descriptions of the rain-soaked streets and the dim glow of streetlights can enhance the atmosphere, making readers feel present with the characters.

Incorporate Sensory Details

Engaging multiple senses can transport readers into the story's world, making experiences feel more real and immersive. When describing a tense moment, consider the sounds, smells, and sights surrounding your characters. Perhaps the distant wail of a siren echoes as Claire races to uncover the truth, or the scent of damp earth fills the air during a pivotal confrontation. These sensory details enrich the narrative, drawing readers deeper into the unfolding drama.

By implementing these techniques in scene structure, you can create a narrative that captivates readers, balancing thrilling suspense with emotional depth. Each scene becomes a vital piece of the larger puzzle, ensuring that your romantic suspense novel resonates long after the final page is turned.

Crafting Distinct Dialogue

Dialogue is a powerful tool in storytelling, especially in romantic suspense, where the interplay of words builds tension, reveals character, and deepens emotional connections. Crafting distinct dialogue is essential for creating authentic and believable characters. Here are key techniques to elevate your dialogue writing.

Creating Unique Voices

Each character should possess a distinct voice that reflects their personality, background, and emotional state. This can be achieved through variations in speech patterns, vocabulary, and regional dialects. A confident protagonist might use assertive language and speak in short, decisive sentences, while a more insecure character may hesitate, relying on filler words or seeking validation. Consider how a character's upbringing influences their dialogue; someone from a wealthy background may use formal language, while a character from a working-class background might employ colloquialisms.

Revealing Personality Through Dialogue

The way a character speaks reveals much about who they are. A witty character might engage in playful banter, showcasing their intelligence and charm, while a more serious character may use terse, clipped sentences that reflect their no-nonsense approach. This contrast enhances the dynamic between characters, particularly in romantic situations where playful teasing can spark attraction.

Natural Information Sharing

Avoid the temptation to dump information through dialogue. Instead, allow characters to share details organically within their conversations. This approach creates tension and reveals relationships without feeling forced. For example, rather than having a character state their backstory outright, consider a scene where they reluctantly reveal it during a moment of vulnerability, perhaps after a shared experience or heated argument. This method maintains narrative flow and deepens the reader's investment in the characters' journeys.

Building Tension Through Subtext

In romantic suspense, dialogue often carries layers of meaning. Characters may not always express their true feelings, leading to misunderstandings or hidden agendas. This subtext creates tension and intrigue. For instance, during a conversation about a seemingly mundane topic, one character might hint at deeper feelings or fears, leaving the other character—and the reader—wondering about their true intentions. This technique keeps readers engaged as they seek to decipher the underlying emotions and motivations driving the characters' interactions.

Expressing Attraction and Chemistry

Dialogue serves as a vital avenue for expressing attraction and building romantic tension. Flirtation, teasing, and intimate conversations help establish chemistry between characters. Playful banter can highlight their compatibility, while a heartfelt confession can deepen their emotional connection. Consider a scene where the characters are forced to work together under stressful circumstances, leading to moments of vulnerability that allow them to share fears and desires. This propels the romantic arc forward and intertwines with the suspenseful elements of the plot.

Utilizing Silence Effectively

Lastly, don't underestimate the power of silence in dialogue. Pauses can convey emotional weight, indicate discomfort, or heighten tension. A moment of silence after a character reveals a secret allows the gravity of the moment to sink in, creating a poignant experience for the reader. For instance, after one character admits to a past trauma, the other might struggle to find the right words, leading to a charged silence that speaks volumes about their emotional connection.

In summary, crafting distinct dialogue is an art that requires attention to character voice, natural information sharing, tension-building subtext, and the expression of attraction. By mastering these techniques, you can create dialogue that advances the plot and immerses readers in the emotional landscape of your romantic suspense novel.

8

ROMANTIC TENSION: A DANCE OF SUSPENSE

Pacing Guidelines

In the intricate dance of romantic suspense, pacing is crucial. Skillfully alternating between romantic and suspenseful scenes keeps readers engaged and deepens the emotional resonance of the narrative. By thoughtfully structuring your scenes, you can create a rhythm that maintains tension while allowing readers to connect with the characters on a personal level.

Alternating Scenes:

A powerful technique is to alternate between high-stakes action sequences and quieter moments of emotional intimacy. For example, after a heart-pounding chase where the protagonist narrowly escapes danger, introduce a scene where they share a serene meal with their love interest. This transition deepens their relationship, revealing vulnerabilities and fostering trust. These quieter moments are essential; they provide space for characters to reflect on their experiences and feelings, ensuring that the romance evolves naturally alongside the suspense.

Natural Transitions:

Transitions between romantic and suspenseful elements should feel fluid. A suspenseful scene can seamlessly lead into a romantic moment as characters process their emotions amidst the chaos. For instance, after a tense confrontation with an antagonist, a character might find solace in their partner's embrace, leading to an intimate moment that underscores their bond. This connection heightens emotional stakes and reinforces the idea that their love serves as a sanctuary amid turmoil.

Interwoven Plots:

Make both the romantic and suspense plots integral to the story. The romantic relationship should complicate the suspense, and vice versa. For example, if the protagonist's love interest is kidnapped, they must confront their feelings while racing against time to save them. This intertwining of plots elevates the stakes, as the protagonist's emotional investment directly influences their decision-making in life-or-death situations. The urgency of the suspense amplifies the romantic tension, creating a compelling narrative that keeps readers invested.

Heightening Stakes:

Connecting conflicts in both arcs can significantly elevate tension. If the protagonist's love interest is threatened, it raises suspense and intensifies the emotional stakes of their relationship. For instance, discovering that their partner is entangled in a dangerous conspiracy can spark conflict that tests their trust and loyalty. This duality of conflict enriches the narrative, offering readers a multi-layered experience that intertwines love and danger.

Dual Climaxes:

Aim to build to dual climaxes where both the romantic and suspenseful arcs peak simultaneously. This ensures a satisfying resolution for both elements of the story. Picture a climactic scene where the protagonist confronts the villain while confessing their love to their partner. This powerful moment resolves the suspense plot and solidifies the emotional journey, leaving readers fulfilled in both aspects of the narrative.

By mastering these pacing guidelines, you can create a harmonious balance between romance and suspense, crafting a narrative that captivates readers from beginning to end. The interplay of emotions and tension will enhance your story while establishing a deep connection with your audience, ensuring they are invested in the characters' journeys every step of the way.

Integration Strategies

In the intricate dance of romantic suspense, seamlessly integrating both elements is essential for crafting a compelling narrative. Effective strategies that intertwine romance and suspense ensure that both arcs enhance one another throughout the story.

One powerful technique is to incorporate a midpoint twist that shifts the dynamics of both romance and suspense. Imagine the protagonist discovering that their love interest has been living under a false identity. This revelation complicates their relationship, creating a rift of trust and emotional turmoil while escalating the suspense plot, as the protagonist grapples with the implications of deception amidst looming danger. Such twists captivate readers and deepen the stakes for both characters.

Complications arising from the intertwining of romance and suspense can further enrich the narrative. Consider a situation where misunderstandings lead to emotional conflict while physical threats loom nearby. Perhaps the protagonist misinterprets a moment of intimacy as betrayal while a shadowy figure stalks them. This layering of conflict creates palpable tension that keeps readers invested in both the characters' emotional journeys and their survival.

Every romantic suspense novel benefits from a 'dark moment,' where characters confront their greatest fears. This moment tests their romantic feelings and their resolve in the face of danger. For example, during a high-stakes confrontation with an antagonist, the protagonist might choose between saving their love interest or pursuing the villain. This choice heightens suspense and serves as a crucible for their relationship, compelling them to confront what they truly value.

As the climax approaches, ensure that both romantic and suspenseful elements converge. Picture a scene where the protagonist faces the antagonist while confessing their true feelings to their love interest. This dual resolution creates a powerful narrative payoff, intertwining the fates of both arcs and leaving readers breathless with anticipation and emotional satisfaction.

Finally, the resolution must tie up both storylines in a way that leaves readers fulfilled. After the climactic confrontation, characters should emerge victorious over external threats and with their romantic relationship solidified. Whether through a heartfelt reunion or a moment of quiet reflection, the resolution should encapsulate the growth of both suspense and romance, ensuring that readers walk away with a sense of closure.

By employing these integration strategies, writers can craft narratives where romance and suspense are intricately woven together, enhancing the overall impact of the story. The balance between these two forces is not just a technique; it's the heartbeat of the romantic suspense genre, inviting readers into a world where love and danger collide in exhilarating ways.

Writing Techniques for Effective Balance

Creating a captivating romantic suspense novel requires a delicate balance between romance and suspense. To achieve this, writers must employ various techniques that engage readers on multiple levels, ensuring both plots progress seamlessly and contribute to a thrilling narrative experience.

Engaging Hooks and Early Introductions

Begin your story with a hook that introduces both romance and suspense. Picture a scene where the protagonist, a resourceful detective, pursues a suspect through a rain-soaked alley. Just as she corners him, she unexpectedly encounters her estranged love interest, who is also investigating a related case. This immediate intertwining of their professional and personal lives sets the stage for a narrative rich in both romance and suspense.

Layering Suspense with Romantic Tension

As the story unfolds, introduce multiple suspects or red herrings within the suspense plot to keep readers guessing. This uncertainty allows the romantic tension to build, as the protagonist grapples with her feelings while trying to discern who can be trusted. For instance, if the love interest harbors a secret that connects him to the mystery, the protagonist may struggle with her growing attraction to him while questioning whether he is part of the danger she faces. This internal conflict adds depth to both arcs, keeping readers invested.

Subplots that Enhance the Main Narrative

Incorporate subplots that enhance both the romantic and suspenseful elements of your story. These subplots should complement the main narrative without overshadowing it. For example, a subplot involving a family secret could deepen the protagonist's emotional stakes, revealing why she struggles to trust her love interest. By layering these conflicts, you enrich the reader's experience, providing more avenues for character development and thematic exploration.

Strategic Clues and Foreshadowing

Weave clues and foreshadowing throughout your story that pay off in both arcs. For instance, subtle hints about the love interest's past may lead to a shocking revelation at the climax, where his true identity is unveiled just as the protagonist faces a life-threatening situation. This strategic revelation heightens suspense and compels the protagonist to confront her feelings, creating a moment where love and danger collide.

Progressive Tension Building

Maintain reader engagement by progressively building tension through alternating high-stakes suspense scenes and intimate romantic moments. After a heart-pounding chase, allow your characters a quiet moment to reflect on their feelings, perhaps sharing a vulnerable conversation that reveals their fears and desires. This contrast between action and intimacy keeps the narrative dynamic, ensuring that readers remain emotionally invested.

Catalysts for Character Development

Include action scenes that serve as catalysts for character development. For instance, a confrontation with a dangerous adversary could force the protagonists to rely on each other, revealing their strengths and vulnerabilities. As they fight side by side, their relationship deepens, demonstrating how external pressures can forge stronger bonds. This interplay between romance and suspense drives the plot forward and enriches the characters' arcs.

Maintaining Mystery Until the Climax

Keep the mystery alive until the climax by revealing information strategically. Allow both arcs to unfold in tandem, leading to a thrilling resolution where romantic and suspenseful elements converge. For example, as the protagonist confronts the antagonist, she might simultaneously confess her true feelings for her love interest, creating a climactic moment that satisfies both narrative threads. This dual climax rewards readers for their investment in both romance and suspense, leaving them fulfilled as they reach the story's conclusion.

By employing these techniques, writers can effectively balance the intricate dance of romance and suspense, crafting narratives that resonate with readers and keep them eagerly turning the pages. The key lies in the artful integration of both elements, ensuring that each enhances the other, ultimately leading to a compelling and satisfying story.

9

CRAFTING SETTING AND ATMOSPHERE

The Role of Setting in Enhancing Mood and Tension

Setting is more than just a backdrop in a romantic suspense novel; it is a vital element that shapes the emotional land-scape of the story. A well-crafted setting can evoke powerful emotions, heighten tension, and create an immersive experience for readers. The interplay between the environment and the characters significantly influences the narrative, making it essential for writers to consider how they utilize setting to enhance both romance and suspense.

Imagine a stormy night, with thunder rumbling ominously in the distance. The heavy rain pelting against the windows mirrors the turmoil within the characters, amplifying the sense of danger and drawing readers into the heart of the suspense. In contrast, a cozy cabin nestled in the woods, complete with a crackling fireplace and soft blankets, offers an intimate setting that nurtures romantic development. The warmth of the fire sharply contrasts with the chill outside, creating a safe haven where characters can explore their feelings. Through sensory details—the smell of rain-soaked earth or the flickering shadows cast by the fire—authors can craft an atmosphere that resonates with readers, making them feel the tension or romance vividly.

The interaction between characters and their surroundings can also reveal their emotional states. A cramped, dimly lit space can evoke feelings of claustrophobia and anxiety, mirroring the characters' struggles. Conversely, a wide-open landscape can symbolize freedom and connection, allowing characters to express their vulnerabilities and desires. The setting takes on a life of its own, influencing the actions and decisions of the protagonists. For instance, a character standing at the edge of a cliff, gazing out over a vast ocean, may feel exhilaration that emboldens them to confront their fears.

Understanding the role of setting in crafting a romantic suspense novel is crucial. It serves as a canvas for the emotional and suspenseful arcs, enhancing reader engagement and investment in the story. By thoughtfully integrating setting into the narrative, writers can elevate their storytelling, creating a rich tapestry that intertwines romance and suspense.

Selecting Complementary Settings for Romance and Suspense

Choosing the right setting for a romantic suspense novel is essential, as it profoundly shapes the emotional and thrilling dynamics of the narrative. The ideal setting must fulfill a dual purpose: enhancing romantic moments while providing fertile ground for suspenseful incidents. This delicate balance is vital for crafting an engaging story.

Consider an abandoned warehouse. At first glance, it may appear to be a purely suspenseful locale, perfect for a heart-pounding chase. Yet, within its shadowy corners, it can also become an unexpected sanctuary for intimacy. Imagine two characters, drawn together by circumstances, discovering solace in a moment of vulnerability amid chaos. The contrast between the looming danger outside and the fragile connection they forge within amplifies both suspense and romance.

When selecting settings, it's vital to consider factors such as location, time period, and cultural context. Each element can significantly influence how both romance and suspense are perceived. For instance, a quaint seaside village may evoke nostalgia and warmth, providing a backdrop for romantic encounters while concealing secrets that lead to thrilling plot twists. Conversely, a bustling city can heighten feelings of isolation, where characters may feel lost among the crowd, intensifying their vulnerability.

Weather conditions also play a critical role in enhancing atmosphere. Picture a foggy evening, where visibility is limited and tension is palpable. The obscured surroundings create unease, making every sound feel amplified. In contrast, bright sunlight can symbolize clarity and hope, serving as a backdrop for characters to express their feelings openly. These environmental cues not only set the mood but also mirror the emotional journeys of the characters.

Ultimately, ensuring that the setting aligns with the characters' emotional arcs is vital for creating a cohesive narrative. As characters navigate romantic entanglements and suspenseful challenges, the setting should reflect their internal struggles and growth. A secluded beach at sunset may prompt a character to confess their feelings, while a crowded party might lead to misunderstandings and heightened tension. By thoughtfully selecting settings that resonate with the characters' experiences, writers can craft a narrative that feels authentic and compelling.

In summary, the choice of setting in a romantic suspense novel is a powerful tool that enhances both the romantic and suspenseful elements of the story. By considering the dual purpose of locations, the impact of weather, and how settings influence character actions, authors can create rich, immersive environments that draw readers into the heart of the narrative. These carefully constructed settings elevate the story and deepen emotional engagement, resulting in a memorable reading experience.

Using Sensory Details to Immerse the Reader

Sensory details are the lifeblood of a romantic suspense novel, transforming mere words into a vivid, immersive experience. By engaging the reader's senses—sight, sound, smell, taste, and touch—authors evoke emotions and create a rich atmosphere that enhances both the romantic and suspenseful elements of the story.

Imagine a scene set in autumn, where the air is crisp and leaves crunch underfoot. Describing the vibrant oranges and reds of the foliage not only paints a picturesque setting but also evokes feelings of nostalgia, creating a perfect backdrop for a romantic encounter. A character might take a deep breath, inhaling the earthy scent of fallen leaves, experiencing peace that sharply contrasts with the tension lurking in the shadows. This juxtaposition heightens the reader's emotional investment, making them aware of the stakes of love and danger.

Sound serves as another powerful tool in crafting sensory details. The distant rumble of thunder can signal an approaching storm, mirroring the turmoil within the characters as they confront their feelings. A character's voice, trembling with tension during a confrontation, amplifies suspense, drawing the reader in closer. The interplay of sound and silence—like the sudden stillness before a climactic moment—creates an atmosphere thick with anticipation.

Smell is often underutilized yet can evoke profound emotional responses. The aroma of rain-soaked earth can transport readers to a moment of vulnerability shared between characters, while the scent of a cozy fireplace evokes feelings of safety and intimacy. By weaving in these sensory elements, authors anchor their readers in the scene, making the emotional stakes feel immediate and real.

Touch also plays a significant role in romantic suspense. The warmth of a hand clasped in fear conveys a deep connection between characters, while the chill of a sudden breeze evokes danger. Describing the rough texture of a wall against a character's back during a tense moment heightens the scene's urgency.

Taste can serve as a subtle yet effective sensory detail. A shared glass of wine during a romantic dinner symbolizes intimacy, while the bitter taste of fear lingers in a character's mouth during a suspenseful encounter. These details enrich the narrative and deepen the reader's emotional engagement.

The writer's ability to weave these sensory details seamlessly into the narrative ultimately enriches the reading experience. By grounding the story in tangible sensations, authors create a world that feels alive, where readers can taste the tension and feel the romance as if it were their own. This immersive quality is essential in a romantic suspense novel, allowing the audience to experience the highs and lows of both love and danger, making for a compelling journey.

10

RESEARCH AND AUTHENTICITY IN ACADEMIC WRITING

The Importance of Thorough Research

In romantic suspense, high stakes and narrative authenticity are essential. Readers expect more than just a captivating love story; they seek a tale that intertwines romance with real-world dangers, emotional stakes, and credible plotlines. Therefore, thorough research is vital.

Establishing credibility starts with a deep exploration of the elements that form your story's backbone. If your plot involves law enforcement or criminal investigations, understanding these intricacies can add layers of realism that resonate with readers. For example, knowledge of criminal profiling can shape your characters' motivations and inform their actions, making them more compelling and enhancing the suspenseful atmosphere.

Technical details related to forensic science or psychological evaluations can further elevate your story. If your plot hinges on a murder investigation, knowing how forensic evidence is collected and analyzed can transform a standard whodunit into a gripping tale. Readers with backgrounds in these fields will appreciate your commitment to accuracy, fostering a bond of trust between you and your audience.

Moreover, the professions of your characters—whether detectives, medical examiners, or psychologists—must reflect accurate protocols and procedures. Achieving this level of detail can be accomplished by consulting professionals or analyzing credible sources. For instance, understanding the protocols followed by a medical examiner during an autopsy can enrich your plot and character development. Engaging with experts not only strengthens your research but also opens doors to unique story angles.

In summary, thorough research is the foundation of credibility in romantic suspense. It enables you to craft a narrative that captivates and resonates with readers who crave authenticity. By grounding your story in realistic portrayals and informed character motivations, you pave the way for a compelling read that stands out in a crowded genre.

Techniques for Fact-Checking and Maintaining Accuracy

In romantic suspense, accuracy is a necessity. Readers crave authenticity, especially when the narrative intertwines with real-world dangers and emotional stakes. To ensure your story resonates with credibility, employ effective techniques for fact-checking and maintaining accuracy throughout your writing process.

One effective strategy is to utilize multiple sources for verification. Relying on a single source can lead to inaccuracies that detract from your story's realism. Seek expert opinions and access primary sources whenever possible. For instance, if your plot revolves around a criminal investigation, consider interviewing law enforcement officials or forensic experts. Their insights can provide invaluable depth to your portrayal of procedures and motivations.

Incorporating a variety of research methods is equally essential. Delve into books, academic journals, and reputable online resources to gain a comprehensive understanding of relevant topics. For example, if your protagonist is a forensic psychologist, reading academic literature on criminal behavior can inform their character development and the plot's progression. This multifaceted approach enriches your narrative and equips you to tackle complex themes with confidence.

To keep your research organized and accessible, maintain detailed notes that are indexed and categorized. This method allows for quick reference during the writing process, helping maintain accuracy and consistency in character actions and plot developments. For instance, if a character needs to explain a technical procedure, having your research at hand ensures that the information is presented correctly and seamlessly integrates into the dialogue.

Engaging with online forums or communities related to specific professions or topics can also enhance your understanding. These platforms often provide a wealth of knowledge and allow you to pose questions directly to experts or enthusiasts. For example, if you're writing about a medical emergency, joining a medical forum could offer insights into trauma response, enriching your narrative with realistic details.

Ultimately, fact-checking is about more than gathering information; it's about weaving that information into your story organically and engagingly. By employing these techniques, you elevate the authenticity of your work and deepen your connection with readers. They will appreciate the effort you've invested in ensuring that every detail, from a character's profession to the intricacies of a suspenseful plot twist, is grounded in reality, allowing them to lose themselves in the world you've created.

Balancing Detail and Pacing

In the realm of romantic suspense, where tension and emotion intertwine, integrating detailed research is pivotal for crafting an authentic narrative. Striking a balance between enriching the story with factual depth and maintaining brisk pacing is essential. The challenge lies in presenting information in a way that enhances the narrative without overwhelming the audience.

To achieve this balance, consider the principle of digestible snippets. Instead of inundating readers with lengthy expositions, present information in smaller, manageable pieces. For instance, if your protagonist is a forensic expert explaining DNA analysis, weave this information into dialogue naturally. During a tense moment, they might say, "The chances of a match are one in a billion if the sample is collected correctly. But if the evidence is contaminated..." This approach informs the reader while propelling the narrative forward.

Another effective strategy involves integrating research through character actions and internal thoughts. Imagine a scene where your protagonist, a detective, is piecing together clues in a dimly lit room. As they examine blood spatter, their mind races with thoughts of forensic science: "Each drop tells a story, a trajectory that could lead to the killer." This internal dialogue provides insight into the character's expertise while building tension and advancing the plot.

Sensory details and emotional reactions are powerful tools for balancing detail and pacing. When introducing a new setting, such as a bustling police precinct or a quiet hospital room, use vivid descriptions that engage the reader's senses. For example, "The sterile scent of antiseptic hung in the air of the hospital, mingling with distant sounds of hushed voices and beeping machines." Such imagery grounds the reader in the scene and evokes emotions that resonate with the unfolding story.

Moreover, every detail in your narrative should serve a purpose, enhancing character development or advancing the plot. If your character's knowledge of criminal profiling is crucial to solving the mystery, reveal it through relevant interactions or decisions. For example, as they analyze a suspect's behavior, they might reflect on their training: "Every twitch, every hesitation could reveal the truth hidden beneath layers of deception." By connecting details to character motivations and actions, you maintain story flow and avoid superfluous information.

Mastering the balance between detail and pacing in your romantic suspense novel is essential for creating an engaging reading experience. By presenting research in digestible snippets, integrating it seamlessly into character actions and thoughts, and ensuring every detail serves a narrative purpose, you can create a story that captivates readers while immersing them in a world rich with realism and emotional depth. This careful orchestration of information will enhance the credibility of your narrative and keep readers eagerly turning the pages, invested in both the romance and the suspense that unfolds.

11

EFFECTIVE REVISION AND EDITING STRATEGIES

Evaluating Your Manuscript

As you begin the revision process, the first step is essential for establishing a solid foundation for your romantic suspense novel. This stage involves assessing the manuscript for plot consistency, character development, and the balance of romantic and suspenseful elements.

Plot Consistency

Start your review by examining the intricacies of your plot. Ensure that all storylines align cohesively, with no contradictions in events or character motivations. For example, if your protagonist uncovers a vital clue about a potential threat, confirm that this revelation aligns with their previous actions. A well-structured plot immerses readers in a thrilling journey without jarring inconsistencies.

Character Arcs

Next, focus on your character arcs. Each character should undergo a believable transformation that reflects their experiences and choices. If your heroine begins as a timid investigator, her journey should show her growth into a confident, determined individual by the climax. This organic development enhances reader engagement and fosters deeper emotional connections.

Balancing Romance and Suspense

In romantic suspense, achieving a delicate balance between romance and suspense is crucial. Both arcs should complement each other without overshadowing one another. If your suspense plot features a gripping murder investigation, ensure that the romantic tension evolves concurrently. Identify areas where one element may dominate and adjust accordingly. If the romance feels rushed or overshadowed by suspense, consider adding scenes that allow the characters to connect emotionally amidst the chaos.

Pacing

Assess the pacing of your manuscript to ensure a smooth flow. The rhythm should vary to maintain reader interest; faster pacing during suspenseful scenes heightens tension, while slower moments during romantic developments create depth. If a thrilling chase scene feels prolonged, intersperse it with brief reflections or dialogue that deepen the characters' relationship.

Subplots

Review all subplots to confirm they enhance the main narrative, contributing to character development or thematic depth. Each subplot should feel integral to the primary storyline, enriching the reader's experience. For example, if your protagonist grapples with a troubled past, weaving in a subplot about reconciling with a family member can add layers to her character while driving the main plot forward.

Resolution Satisfaction

Conclude your evaluation by checking for resolution satisfaction. Ensure that both the romantic and suspense plots reach conclusions that resonate with readers. If your characters face a climactic showdown with the antagonist, the aftermath should reflect their growth and the evolution of their relationship. A well-rounded resolution leaves readers feeling fulfilled and eager to recommend your novel.

By focusing on these strategies during your evaluation, you lay the groundwork for a polished manuscript that captivates readers and meets the expectations of the romantic suspense genre. Each element you refine contributes to a compelling narrative, drawing readers into a world where love and danger intertwine seamlessly.

Once you have evaluated your manuscript for plot consistency and character arcs, it's time to move on to the second pass: polishing your prose. This stage is crucial for refining the narrative and ensuring that your story resonates with readers on an emotional level. Here are key strategies to enhance your writing:

Tightening Dialogue for Authenticity

Dialogue is vital to your characters, offering insight into their personalities, motivations, and relationships. Examine each conversation for naturalness. Each character should have a distinct voice that reflects their background. For instance, a seasoned detective might speak in clipped, direct phrases, while a romantic interest could be more whimsical. Remove unnecessary filler that does not advance the plot or deepen character development. If a line doesn't serve a purpose, cut it to create more engaging and authentic dialogue.

Adding Sensory Details

To immerse your readers, incorporate sensory details throughout your manuscript. Engage all five senses—sight, sound, smell, taste, and touch. Instead of simply stating that a character walked into a café, describe the rich aroma of freshly brewed coffee mingling with the scent of pastries, the chatter of patrons, and the warmth of sunlight streaming through the windows. This not only paints a vivid picture but also evokes emotions that resonate with your audience, drawing them deeper into the narrative.

Enhancing Descriptions for Clarity and Depth

While vivid imagery is important, balance is key. Avoid over-describing; aim for clarity and depth that keeps the story moving. Use metaphors and similes to elevate your descriptions. For instance, instead of saying "the storm was strong," you might say, "the storm raged like a wild beast, tearing through the night with a ferocity that rattled the windows." This conveys intensity while adding an emotional layer to the scene.

Checking Transitions Between Scenes

Smooth transitions are essential for maintaining narrative flow. As you move from one scene to the next, ensure that shifts in time, location, or perspective feel natural. For example, if you shift from a tense confrontation to an intimate moment between protagonists, use a subtle cue—a lingering glance or a shared breath—to bridge the two scenes seamlessly. This keeps readers engaged and invested in the emotional journey of your characters.

Verifying Tension in the Plot

Every scene should contribute to escalating tension, whether through external threats or internal conflicts. As you polish your prose, check that both romantic and suspenseful aspects of the plot are intertwined and progressing. If your protagonist is on the run from a mysterious figure, ensure their romantic moments are laced with urgency—perhaps they share a passionate kiss before fleeing, heightening both the stakes and the emotional connection. This dual tension keeps readers on edge, eager to see how both arcs unfold.

By focusing on these elements during your revision, you will refine your manuscript into a polished, engaging work that captivates readers. Each sentence should resonate with authenticity, every description should evoke emotion, and all dialogue should reflect the unique voices of your characters. As you continue to hone your prose, remember that this process is not just about correcting errors; it's about elevating your story to its fullest potential.

Final Pass: Finishing Touches

As you approach the final stages of your manuscript, focus on the finishing touches that will elevate your romantic suspense novel from a rough draft to a polished piece ready for publication. This final pass is where the magic happens, ensuring that every word resonates with your readers and captivates from start to finish.

Conduct a Thorough Grammar and Spelling Check

Even small grammatical errors can disrupt the flow of your narrative. Begin by meticulously combing through your manuscript for spelling and grammatical mistakes. While digital tools can help, don't rely solely on them. Reading your manuscript aloud is a powerful technique to catch errors that software might miss. This practice allows you to hear the rhythm of your prose and identify awkward phrases or incorrect word usage. If a character's dialogue feels stilted when spoken, it's a sign that it needs refinement.

Verify Formatting to Meet Publication Standards

Formatting plays a crucial role in readability and professionalism. Ensure that your manuscript adheres to industry standards: consistent font type and size, uniform line spacing, and clear chapter breaks are vital. A well-formatted document not only looks polished but also enhances the reading experience, making it easier for agents, editors, and readers to engage with your story.

Review Chapter Breaks for Engagement

Every chapter serves as a stepping stone in your narrative, and the way you conclude each one is pivotal. Aim to end chapters with hooks or intriguing questions that leave readers eager to turn the page. For instance, if your suspenseful plot involves a mysterious disappearance, concluding a chapter with your protagonist receiving an anonymous message can create anticipation. This technique keeps the momentum going and ensures that readers remain invested in both the romantic and suspenseful threads of your story.

Check Scene Transitions for Fluidity

The transitions between scenes and chapters should feel seamless, guiding readers effortlessly through your narrative. Each scene should logically lead into the next, maintaining continuity in action and character emotions. If you shift from a tense confrontation to a tender moment between protagonists, ensure that the emotional flow feels natural. For example, after a high-stakes chase, transitioning to a quiet moment where the characters reflect on their feelings can provide a poignant contrast that deepens their connection.

Verify Continuity in Character Behaviors and Plot Details

Consistency is key in character development and plot progression. Review your characters to ensure they behave in accordance with their established traits throughout the story. If a character has been portrayed as cautious, ensure their actions align with that trait, especially during moments of high tension. Similarly, plot details should remain coherent; if a character discovers a crucial clue, ensure that it logically fits within the story's framework.

Polish the Opening and Ending of the Manuscript

The opening of your manuscript is your first impression—make it count. It should grab readers' attention immediately, drawing them into the world you've created. Consider starting with an action-packed scene or a tantalizing glimpse of the romantic tension to come. Conversely, the ending should provide a satisfying resolution that resonates emotionally. Reflect on how your characters have grown and how their journeys culminate in a rewarding way. A powerful final line can linger in the reader's mind long after they've closed the book.

Assess Marketability

Finally, consider the marketability of your manuscript. Familiarize yourself with current trends in the romantic suspense genre. Are there particular themes, tropes, or character archetypes resonating with readers? Ensure that your manuscript aligns with reader expectations in terms of pacing, character development, and thematic depth. This awareness can significantly impact how your work is received.

By focusing on these strategies during your final pass, you can refine your manuscript into a polished, engaging work that meets both reader expectations and industry standards. This is your chance to shine—give your romantic suspense novel the attention it deserves and prepare to captivate your audience.

12

MARKET CONSIDERATIONS AND STRATEGIC INSIGHTS

Current Trends in Romantic Suspense

The romantic suspense genre is experiencing a vibrant resurgence, captivating readers with its unique blend of thrill and emotional depth. For aspiring authors, understanding current trends is essential for crafting stories that resonate with audiences.

One of the most popular subgenres today is the psychological thriller. These narratives delve into the minds of antagonists, creating a chilling atmosphere that heightens suspense. Readers are drawn to the complexity of characters whose motivations remain shrouded in mystery, leading to an immersive experience where the line between love and danger blurs. Novels like *The Girl on the Train* by Paula Hawkins exemplify this trend, intertwining a gripping psychological plot with profound emotional stakes.

Another emerging trend is the cozy mystery, which infuses light-hearted romantic elements into the thrill of solving a crime. These stories often feature amateur sleuths who navigate their personal lives while unraveling mysteries. A prime example is the *The No. 1 Ladies' Detective Agency* series by Alexander McCall Smith, where the charm of the setting and relationships enhances the suspense without overwhelming the reader. This approach appeals to those seeking a balance between tension and warmth.

Dark romantic suspense is also gaining traction, exploring taboo themes and intense emotional connections between characters. These narratives delve into the darker aspects of love and desire, compelling readers to confront their fears. Books like *The Darkest Night* by Gena Showalter illustrate this trend, where the interplay of passion and peril creates a gripping reading experience.

Additionally, genres such as paranormal romance and historical romantic suspense are becoming increasingly popular, reflecting diverse reader interests. Paranormal elements introduce an otherworldly twist, while historical settings provide a rich backdrop for suspenseful narratives. Each of these subgenres offers unique opportunities for authors to explore the complexities of love amidst danger.

Understanding reader preferences is crucial in this evolving landscape. Many readers seek a harmonious blend of suspense and romance, where the thrill of the chase is matched by the emotional stakes of the characters' relationships. This balance ensures that stories not only keep readers on the edge of their seats but also tug at their heartstrings.

As you embark on your journey to write a bestselling romantic suspense novel, keep these trends in mind. By weaving together elements that resonate with contemporary readers, you can create a narrative that stands out in a crowded market, capturing the hearts and imaginations of your audience. Embrace the richness of the genre, and let your creativity flourish as you explore the thrilling intersection of romance and suspense.

Industry Standards and Expectations

As you write a bestselling romantic suspense novel, it is essential to grasp the industry standards and expectations that define this dynamic genre. Navigating these parameters will enhance your chances of publication and ensure that your work resonates with your target audience.

Length Requirements:

Most publishers in the romantic suspense arena expect manuscripts to fall within 70,000 to 100,000 words. This range accommodates the intricate plotting and character development that the genre demands. However, specific subgenres may have different expectations. For instance, psychological thrillers may lean toward the higher end due to their complex narratives, while cozy mysteries might fit comfortably within the lower range. Understanding these nuances will help you tailor your manuscript to meet industry standards.

Heat Levels:

The level of sensuality in your romantic suspense novel is another critical aspect to consider. Readers have diverse preferences; some enjoy closed-door encounters, where intimacy is suggested rather than explicitly described, while others crave steamy interactions. Familiarizing yourself with your target audience's expectations regarding heat levels will guide you in crafting a romantic arc that feels both authentic and engaging.

Plot Complexity:

A well-structured plot is the backbone of any successful romantic suspense novel. Your story should seamlessly intertwine suspense and romance, maintaining tension while developing a believable romantic arc. Publishers look for narratives that keep readers on the edge of their seats, with twists and turns that surprise and delight. For example, a plot that begins with a murder investigation can evolve into a layered exploration of the protagonists' emotional vulnerabilities, creating a compelling dual narrative.

Series Potential:

In an era where readers crave immersive experiences, many publishers favor novels that can develop into a series. This approach allows for deeper character and world-building across multiple installments, providing readers with a sense of continuity and connection. If your characters resonate with audiences, consider how their journeys could unfold over several books, exploring new conflicts and romantic developments in each installment.

Understanding these industry standards and expectations is essential for aspiring authors in the romantic suspense genre. By adhering to length requirements, gauging heat levels, crafting complex plots, and considering series potential, you can position your work for success in a competitive marketplace. Embrace these guidelines as you write and let them inspire you to create a manuscript that captivates readers.

Publishing Options for Aspiring Authors

Navigating the publishing landscape can be daunting for aspiring authors in the romantic suspense genre. With the right approach, you can find a path that aligns with your goals and maximizes your potential for success. Here, we'll explore three primary publishing options: traditional publishing, self-publishing, and a hybrid approach, each offering unique benefits and challenges.

Traditional Publishing

For many writers, traditional publishing represents the gold standard. This route typically involves submitting your manuscript to established publishing houses, which provide invaluable resources such as professional editing, marketing, and distribution. However, securing a contract can be competitive, often requiring a well-crafted query letter and a polished manuscript.

To increase your chances of acceptance, it's essential to build a strong author platform. This includes developing an online presence through social media, creating a personal website, and engaging with potential readers. Networking within the industry—by attending writing conferences, joining writer groups, and connecting with agents—can also open doors to new opportunities. Keep in mind that most publishers prefer manuscripts that fall within the industry standards of 70,000 to 100,000 words, ensuring your story is concise yet impactful.

Self-Publishing

Self-publishing has revolutionized the way authors share their stories, granting them greater control over their creative process. This option allows you to publish your work on platforms like Amazon Kindle Direct Publishing or IngramSpark, where you can set your own pricing and retain a higher percentage of royalties. However, self-publishing comes with its own responsibilities, including editing, cover design, and marketing.

Successful self-published authors often engage in extensive platform building to connect with their audience. This may involve creating a mailing list, participating in book promotions, and actively using social media to generate buzz about their books. The flexibility of self-publishing enables you to experiment with different heat levels and subgenres, tailoring your work to meet the diverse preferences of your readers.

Hybrid Approach

The hybrid publishing model combines the best of both worlds, allowing authors to maximize their reach and income. This strategy might involve publishing your main works through traditional means while self-publishing shorter pieces, novellas, or spin-off stories that expand your universe or delve deeper into supporting characters.

By adopting a hybrid approach, you can enjoy the benefits of professional support from traditional publishers while also exploring your creative freedom through self-publishing. This flexibility enables you to adapt to market trends and reader preferences, ensuring that your work remains relevant and engaging.

Regardless of the path you choose, effective marketing strategies are vital for engaging readers and enhancing visibility in a crowded marketplace. Whether you're crafting an enticing blurb or leveraging social media, the right marketing approach can make all the difference in attracting your target audience.

Understanding your publishing options is crucial as you embark on your journey in romantic suspense. Each route offers unique advantages, and by carefully considering your goals and resources, you can select the path that best suits your aspirations as an author. Embrace the journey ahead, and remember that every step brings you closer to sharing your captivating stories with the world.

13

AVOIDING COMMON PITFALLS

Story Issues

In romantic suspense, achieving a delicate balance between romance and suspense is essential. A successful novel in this genre relies on this equilibrium; if one element overshadows the other, the narrative can become disjointed, leaving readers unfulfilled. For instance, a story that focuses too heavily on romance may lack the tension needed to engage readers, while a narrative centered solely on suspense may neglect character development, making it difficult for readers to invest emotionally. Striking the right balance enriches both arcs, creating a more immersive reading experience.

A compelling suspense plot is crucial for sustaining reader interest. Avoid predictable twists and scenarios that fail to captivate. Instead, introduce complex, high-stakes situations that challenge your characters and keep readers on edge. Incorporate elements such as murder investigations, conspiracies, or hidden identities. These components heighten suspense and deepen the characters' motivations and relationships, seamlessly intertwining the romantic and suspenseful threads.

The romantic arc should emerge naturally from the characters' interactions and shared experiences. Forced romance—where the love story feels contrived—can disengage readers. For example, if two characters come together solely because the plot demands it, rather than due to organic chemistry, their connection may feel hollow. Allow the romance to blossom through shared trials and tribulations, complicated by the suspenseful elements of the plot. This organic evolution of feelings creates a more authentic love story.

Pacing is another critical aspect. The rhythm of your narrative must allow both romance and suspense to flourish. Rapid shifts can confuse readers, while slow pacing may lead to disinterest. Utilize quieter moments to develop relationships and gradually escalate tension. For instance, after a high-stakes chase scene, a reflective moment between the protagonists can deepen their bond and heighten the stakes of their relationship. Ensure that both plots progress in tandem, allowing readers to feel the weight of both the romantic and suspenseful arcs.

Moreover, the situations you present must remain realistic. Readers are drawn to believable scenarios, so avoid events that defy logic or are overly dramatic without justification. Characters should react realistically to the stakes at hand, preserving the story's credibility. If a character suddenly demonstrates an improbable skill or knowledge without prior development, it can disrupt readers' immersion.

Finally, ensure that both the romantic and suspense elements reach a satisfying conclusion. A resolution that feels rushed or unearned can leave readers dissatisfied. Take the time to develop character growth and plot developments that culminate in a logical and impactful ending. For example, if your protagonists have battled through emotional barriers and external dangers, their resolution should reflect that journey, providing closure that resonates with the reader.

In summary, avoiding common story issues is vital for crafting a successful romantic suspense novel. Focus on creating a balanced narrative that intertwines romance and suspense, developing multidimensional characters whose arcs evolve naturally, and ensuring that the technical aspects of your story are executed with care. By doing so, you will engage readers and deliver a compelling story that lingers long after the last page is turned.

Character Issues

Creating compelling characters is essential for any successful romantic suspense novel. When characters lack depth or authenticity, the entire narrative suffers, leaving readers disengaged. Here are common character-related pitfalls to avoid, ensuring your protagonists and antagonists resonate with readers.

Stereotypical Characters

One significant misstep in character development is relying on clichés. Readers crave depth and relatability, so it's vital to craft nuanced protagonists and antagonists. Instead of a typical "damsel in distress," consider a female lead who is a skilled investigator grappling with her own past traumas. This complexity enriches her character and makes her journey more compelling. Avoiding stereotypes enhances emotional impact and fosters a stronger connection with your audience.

Lack of Chemistry

The chemistry between romantic leads is crucial in a romantic suspense novel. If the attraction feels forced, readers may struggle to invest in the relationship. Take the time to develop their interactions through shared experiences, intimate conversations, and moments of vulnerability. Imagine a scene where the characters are trapped together in a dangerous situation, leading to heightened emotions and a natural blossoming of their relationship. This organic development of chemistry keeps readers engaged.

Unrealistic Abilities

Characters should possess skills that align with their backgrounds and roles in the story. Avoid creating protagonists who seem too perfect or have abilities that do not realistically fit the narrative. If your lead is a detective, ensure she has the training and experience to handle high-stakes situations. For instance, if she suddenly performs a complex hacking maneuver without prior knowledge, it can break immersion. Instead, allow her skills to evolve naturally through the plot, showcasing her growth while maintaining believability.

Poor Motivation

Every character should have clear motivations driving their actions. Readers need to understand why a character behaves a certain way. For example, if your lead is a journalist investigating a conspiracy, her motivation could stem from a personal loss tied to the events she's uncovering. Weak motivation can lead to inconsistent behavior, confusing readers and undermining character arcs. By grounding your characters' goals in relatable experiences, you create a more cohesive narrative.

Inconsistent Behavior

Consistency in character behavior is vital for maintaining reader trust. Characters should act in ways that are true to their established personalities and motivations. Sudden shifts in behavior can alienate readers and disrupt the story's flow. For instance, if your protagonist is portrayed as cautious and analytical, a sudden impulsive decision without proper buildup can feel jarring. Develop characters with relatable flaws and strengths that evolve naturally throughout the narrative, allowing for growth while maintaining their core essence.

Weak Antagonist

A compelling antagonist is essential for creating tension and conflict. Avoid flat or one-dimensional villains. Instead, develop a strong antagonist with their own motivations and complexities. Consider a villain who is not just evil for the sake of being evil but has a tragic backstory that informs their actions. This depth makes the conflict more engaging and multifaceted, allowing readers to understand the antagonist's perspective, even if they don't agree with it.

Avoiding these common character-related pitfalls is crucial for crafting a successful romantic suspense novel. Focus on creating multidimensional characters with relatable motivations, authentic chemistry, and consistent behavior. By doing so, you will engage readers on an emotional level, drawing them into the intricate web of romance and suspense that defines your story.

Technical Issues

In the world of romantic suspense, technical issues can undermine the narrative, leaving readers disengaged. Writers must remain vigilant about the technical aspects of storytelling to create a seamless experience. Below are common pitfalls to avoid, along with strategies to enhance your writing.

Info Dumping

One significant misstep is overwhelming readers with excessive exposition. Info dumping—providing large amounts of background information all at once—can disrupt the narrative flow. Instead of presenting character histories or plot details through lengthy descriptions, strive to integrate this information organically. For instance, reveal a character's traumatic past through their reactions in a high-stakes situation rather than through a tedious monologue. Show, don't tell; let readers discover the layers of your characters and story as they unfold.

Poor Research

Authenticity is vital in romantic suspense, particularly regarding settings and procedures. Conduct thorough research; it is a necessity. Readers are drawn to believable scenarios, and inaccuracies can distract from the story's impact. For example, if your plot involves a murder investigation, ensure that the depicted procedures align with real law enforcement practices. Misinformation can break the reader's trust and diminish investment in the narrative. Verify details through books, interviews with professionals, or credible online resources.

Unrealistic Procedures

In addition to general research, pay close attention to the accuracy of specific procedures related to law enforcement or other professional fields. Readers familiar with these areas will notice discrepancies, detracting from the suspenseful elements of your story. If your protagonist is a detective, ensure their investigative methods reflect realistic practices. This authenticity enhances credibility and enriches the reader's experience.

Weak Dialogue

Dialogue is a powerful tool for revealing character traits, advancing the plot, and building tension. Yet, weak dialogue can hinder these objectives. Avoid stilted or overly formal language that doesn't feel true to the characters. Instead, strive for authenticity by giving each character a distinct voice that reflects their personality and background. For example, a seasoned detective might use concise, no-nonsense language, while a romantic lead could express themselves more poetically. Utilize dialogue to create moments of intimacy, conflict, and revelation, ensuring it feels natural and engaging.

Poor Transitions

Smooth transitions between scenes and chapters are crucial for maintaining narrative flow. Abrupt shifts can jar the reader and disrupt immersion. To create seamless transitions, ensure that changes in time or perspective feel organic. For instance, if you're shifting from a tense confrontation to a quieter moment, consider using a shared memory or sensory detail to bridge the two scenes. This technique enhances continuity and deepens the emotional resonance of the narrative.

Pacing Problems

Pacing is essential for keeping readers engaged. Monitor the rhythm of your manuscript to avoid sections that drag or feel rushed. A well-paced story fosters romance and suspense, creating a dynamic reading experience. Use varied sentence structures to maintain momentum, alternating between action and introspection. For instance, follow a heart-pounding chase scene with a moment of quiet reflection for your characters, allowing readers to process the tension while deepening their connection to the protagonists.

Avoiding these common technical pitfalls is crucial for crafting a compelling romantic suspense novel. By focusing on creating an engaging narrative through the seamless integration of information, thorough research, authentic dialogue, smooth transitions, and careful pacing, you can enhance the reader's experience and deliver a story that resonates deeply. Remember, the goal is to immerse your audience in a world where romance and suspense coexist, drawing them into the emotional journey of your characters while keeping them on the edge of their seats.

14

UNLOCKING THE SECRETS TO SUCCESS IN ROMANTIC SUSPENSE

Writing Quality

The cornerstone of any bestselling romantic suspense novel is the quality of writing. This genre requires a unique blend of gripping storytelling and emotional depth, which hinges on several key elements.

Strong Opening: Your novel must begin with a hook that captures the reader's attention immediately. Consider opening with the protagonist thrust into a perilous situation, establishing suspense and piquing interest in the romantic arc. For instance, a character witnessing a crime during a seemingly mundane evening sets the stage for both danger and romantic entanglement.

Engaging Characters: Characters should be multi-dimensional, with relatable flaws and compelling motivations.

Protagonists need to evoke empathy, allowing readers to invest emotionally in their journeys. A skilled detective grappling with her past might find herself drawn to a charming yet mysterious stranger harboring secrets. Their interactions should reveal complexities and create palpable chemistry that draws readers deeper into the narrative.

Tight Plotting: A well-structured plot maintains momentum and keeps readers on edge. Each chapter should serve a purpose, whether advancing suspense or deepening the romantic connection. Layering subplots—such as a personal vendetta or a family secret—can heighten stakes and enrich character development.

Natural Dialogue: Dialogue must feel authentic and advance both the plot and character relationships. It should reflect the characters' personalities and the tension in their situations. A heated exchange during a moment of danger can reveal vulnerabilities and deepen emotional connections, making the romance feel more earned and impactful.

Vivid Descriptions: Immersive descriptions transport readers into your story. Use sensory details to evoke atmosphere—whether the tension in a dimly lit alley or the warmth of a shared moment in a cozy café. This enhances the setting and allows readers to feel the characters' emotions more acutely.

Emotional Depth: Emotional resonance is crucial. Readers should feel the stakes in both suspense and romance. Show characters' vulnerabilities, fears, and desires as they navigate challenges. A scene where the couple confronts their fears together can create a powerful moment of connection, reinforcing the theme of love prevailing amidst chaos.

Satisfying Ending: A fulfilling conclusion provides closure for both romantic and suspenseful arcs. Ensure both plots resolve in a way that satisfies reader expectations. For example, protagonists might overcome external threats while addressing personal conflicts, leading to a resolution that feels earned and authentic.

Writing quality in romantic suspense hinges on crafting a compelling opening, developing engaging characters, maintaining tight plotting, creating natural dialogue, using vivid descriptions, and delivering emotional depth. By focusing on these elements, writers can create stories that resonate deeply with readers, ensuring a satisfying experience that lingers long after the final page.

Market Awareness

Understanding the market landscape is essential for any writer aspiring to succeed in the romantic suspense genre. As trends evolve and reader preferences shift, staying informed can make the difference between a book that resonates with audiences and one that fades into obscurity. Here are essential strategies for developing market awareness.

First, it is vital to stay current with romantic suspense trends. This genre encompasses various subgenres, from cozy mysteries to darker thrillers, each appealing to different reader demographics. A recent survey by the Romance Writers of America revealed that readers increasingly prefer stories incorporating elements of psychological suspense and character-driven plots. Understanding which subgenres are gaining popularity can help you tailor your work to meet reader desires.

Moreover, length requirements and heat level expectations are critical factors to consider. Many publishers have specific guidelines regarding word count and the intensity of romantic scenes. For instance, traditional publishers often prefer manuscripts between 70,000 and 90,000 words for romantic suspense novels. Additionally, heat levels can vary; some readers seek steamy encounters, while others prefer a more subdued approach. Familiarizing yourself with these nuances will enable you to position your story effectively within the market.

Developing a marketing plan is another essential component of market awareness. In today's digital age, building an author platform is crucial. This can include creating a professional website to showcase your work, engaging with readers through social media, and maintaining a newsletter that shares insights, updates, and exclusive content. Authors who regularly interact with their audience on platforms like

Instagram or Facebook often see increased engagement and loyalty from their readers.

Furthermore, understanding your publishing options can significantly impact your career trajectory. Whether you choose traditional publishing, a small press, self-publishing, or a hybrid approach, each path has its own advantages and challenges. Traditional publishing may offer broader distribution and marketing support, while self-publishing allows for greater creative control and potentially higher royalties. Researching and evaluating these options ensures you select the best route for your work, aligning with your goals and vision as an author.

Leveraging marketing hooks to attract potential readers is essential. Crafting a compelling elevator pitch highlighting your story's unique aspects can pique interest and draw readers in. For example, if your romantic suspense novel features a protagonist with a hidden past intertwined with a thrilling murder investigation, emphasizing this duality in your promotional materials can create intrigue and encourage readers to pick up your book.

Maintaining market awareness is a multifaceted endeavor that requires continuous learning and adaptation. By staying informed about trends, understanding reader expectations, developing a robust marketing strategy, and exploring various publishing routes, you can position yourself for success in the competitive world of romantic suspense. Focus on creating quality stories that satisfy both romantic and suspenseful elements while remaining engaged with the literary community and its ever-changing dynamics.

Professional Development

In the ever-evolving world of romantic suspense, continuous learning is essential for writers seeking to refine their craft and achieve success. The writer's journey goes beyond putting words on a page; it involves engaging with a community, acquiring knowledge, and fostering personal growth. By immersing themselves in professional development, authors can elevate their skills and enhance their narratives.

One effective way to improve your writing is by joining writing organizations. These groups offer invaluable resources, including workshops, webinars, and critique opportunities that sharpen storytelling abilities. For example, organizations like the Romance Writers of America (RWA) provide a wealth of information tailored for romance authors, including access to industry insights and networking opportunities.

Attending conferences is another crucial avenue for professional growth. Events such as the RWA National Conference enable writers to connect with industry professionals and learn from successful authors who have navigated the complexities of publishing. These gatherings foster collaboration and support, where aspiring writers can share experiences, gain encouragement, and build relationships that may lead to mentorship or collaboration on future projects.

In addition to networking, studying craft books and reading extensively are fundamental practices for any writer. Works like "Save the Cat! Writes a Novel" by Jessica Brody and "The Emotion Thesaurus" by Angela Ackerman and Becca Puglisi provide insights into narrative techniques, character development, and emotional depth. By absorbing these resources, writers can gain a deeper understanding of storytelling mechanics and apply these lessons to their work. Seeking professional feedback from editors or writing coaches can also offer critical insights that refine a manuscript, enhancing its overall quality and appeal.

Participating in writing workshops or critique groups can be particularly beneficial. These settings allow writers to share their work in a supportive environment, receiving constructive feedback that illuminates strengths and weaknesses in their narratives. Engaging in this process fosters improvement and builds confidence in one's writing abilities.

Professional development is a continuous journey that requires commitment and dedication. By actively participating in writing organizations, attending conferences, studying the craft, and seeking feedback, authors can cultivate their skills and deepen their understanding of the romantic suspense genre. This dedication to growth enhances the quality of their writing and enriches their storytelling, ultimately leading to more compelling and successful novels. Embrace the journey, and let each step forward be a testament to your passion for the craft.

15

FINAL THOUGHTS

Writing a romantic suspense novel transcends mere storytelling; it is a profound journey of learning, growth, and self-discovery. Aspiring authors must recognize that every writer, regardless of their level of experience, encounters challenges along the way. The road to success in this genre, which intricately blends romance with suspense, is often fraught with obstacles. Yet, persistence is the cornerstone of achieving true success.

Bestselling authors have navigated the peaks and valleys of the writing landscape, facing rejections, self-doubt, and frustration. However, their unwavering passion for storytelling and dedication to their craft have propelled them forward. Take Tessa Bailey, for example; she transformed her love for romantic suspense into a thriving career despite facing numerous early setbacks. Her journey exemplifies the power of resilience and the importance of embracing the process, no matter how intimidating it may appear.

As you embark on your writing journey, remember that every word you write brings you closer to uncovering your unique voice and style. Approach writing not just as a hobby, but as both a passion and a profession. Allow your creativity to flourish while refining your skills through practice and constructive feedback. Participate in writing workshops or online forums to share your work and gain insights from fellow writers. This collaborative spirit can be incredibly enriching and will aid your growth as a storyteller.

Embrace the learning process and seize every opportunity to expand your knowledge of the craft. Whether through extensive reading in the genre, studying craft books, or attending seminars, each experience contributes to your development as a writer. The more you immerse yourself in romantic suspense, the better equipped you will be to create stories that resonate with readers.

Ultimately, the journey of writing a romantic suspense novel is as significant as the destination. It invites you to explore your creativity, confront your fears, and delve into the depths of your imagination. By remaining passionate and committed, you will not only enhance your craft but also cultivate a deep connection with your characters and readers. Embrace the journey; it is within this process that you will discover the heart of your storytelling.

. . .

Building Your Network

In the writing world, the adage "it's not what you know, but who you know" rings particularly true. For aspiring writers, especially those venturing into romantic suspense, building a robust network is crucial. The connections you forge can provide invaluable insights, support, and opportunities that propel your writing career forward.

A highly effective way to start is by joining writing organizations. Groups like the Romance Writers of America (RWA) or local writing clubs offer a wealth of resources, including workshops, webinars, and meet-ups. Attending an RWA conference not only grants access to industry professionals but also fosters a sense of community among writers who share your passion.

Conferences and workshops serve as fertile ground for networking. Engaging in discussions, asking questions, and sharing your work can open doors to new relationships. You might meet a fellow writer who becomes a critique partner or a published author willing to share their journey and offer guidance. These connections can lead to collaborations, mentorships, and friendships that enrich your writing experience.

In addition to formal organizations, online communities have flourished, providing platforms for global connections.

Engaging on social media platforms like X (formerly Twitter), Instagram, Facebook, TikTok, or dedicated writing forums can extend your reach beyond geographical boundaries. Participating in writing challenges or using hashtags like #amwriting or #RomSuspense introduces you to diverse voices and perspectives. Sharing your journey online builds confidence and attracts followers who resonate with your work.

Consider attending local book signings or author readings. These events are not just for readers; they present prime opportunities for writers to mingle with authors, agents, and publishers. Engaging in conversations about their works can yield insights into the industry and open doors to future collaborations. Remember, each interaction is a chance to learn and grow.

As you build your network, prioritize reciprocity. Networking is not solely about what you can gain; it's equally about what you can offer. Share your knowledge, provide feedback, and support your peers. This mutual exchange fosters a positive environment where everyone can thrive.

In a competitive market, a strong author platform is essential. Your network enhances your visibility and credibility. By actively participating in your writing community, you position yourself as a serious author engaged in the craft. This visibility can lead to opportunities such as guest blogging, speaking engagements, and even publishing deals.

Building your network is a vital step in your journey as a romantic suspense writer. Embrace the opportunities that arise, engage with fellow writers, and immerse yourself in the community. Each connection you make holds the potential to lead to new horizons in your writing career. With persistence and passion, you can cultivate a network that supports your growth as a writer and enriches your journey in the captivating world of romantic suspense.

Confidence in Your Craft

As you set out to write a bestselling romantic suspense novel, cultivating confidence in your craft is essential. This confidence is not merely a belief in your abilities; it is a deep understanding that your unique voice and perspective are valuable contributions to the genre. Recognizing that authenticity and originality are the cornerstones of a compelling story empowers you to express your thoughts and emotions freely.

To nurture this confidence, immerse yourself in literature. Read widely within and beyond the romantic suspense genre. Analyze the works of authors you admire—what techniques do they employ to create tension, develop characters, or build romance? Studying their craft can provide insights that resonate with your own writing style. Consider the emotional depth of a book like "The Witness" by Nora Roberts, where the intricate blend of suspense and romance keeps readers on the edge of their seats. Reflect on what you can learn from her character development and pacing.

Delve into craft books that offer practical advice and strategies for writers. Titles such as "Writing Down the Bones" by Natalie Goldberg or "Save the Cat! Writes a Novel" by Jessica Brody provide valuable frameworks to help refine your storytelling abilities. These resources can guide you in structuring your plot, developing characters, and enhancing dialogue—elements vital for success in romantic suspense.

Seeking professional feedback is another crucial step in building your confidence. Sharing your work with trusted peers or joining a writing group can offer fresh perspectives and constructive criticism. Embrace feedback as an opportunity for growth. Remember, even the most successful authors have faced rejection and criticism. Multiple publishers famously rejected J.K. Rowling's "Harry Potter" series before it became a global phenomenon. Let her journey remind you that persistence, coupled with a willingness to learn, can lead to extraordinary outcomes.

Accepting that mistakes and setbacks are part of the learning process is vital for resilience. Every writer encounters challenges—be it writer's block, plot holes, or character inconsistencies. Rather than viewing these obstacles as failures, see them as stepping stones to improvement. Each draft you write and each revision you undertake brings you closer to mastering your craft. Embrace the idea that growth comes from pushing through difficulties, and allow yourself the grace to evolve as a writer.

Ultimately, believing in your ability to create engaging narratives and connect with readers is fundamental to achieving success in romantic suspense. Your stories have the potential to resonate deeply, evoking emotions and provoking thought. As you write, visualize your ideal reader and the impact your words will have on them. Picture the thrill of a reader turning the pages late into the night, captivated by the romance and suspense you've woven together.

In this genre, where love intertwines with danger, your voice matters. Trust in your journey, embrace the learning curve, and know that with each word you write, you are one step closer to crafting a story that entertains and leaves a lasting impression on your readers. Your confidence will shine through in your writing, and as you continue to hone your skills, you will find your place in the vibrant world of romantic suspense.